BREAKING RANK

BREAKING RANK

Kristen D. Randle

Morrow Junior Books

New York

Published by Morrow Junior Books
a division of William Morrow and Company, Inc.
1350 Avenue of the Americas, New York, NY 10019
www.williammorrow.com

Printed in the United States of America.

10 9 8 7 6 5 4 3 2 1

Library of Congress Cataloging-in-Publication Data
Randle, Kristen D.
Breaking rank / Kristen D. Randle.
p. cm.
Summary: Seventeen-year-old Casey has some of her preconceived
notions challenged when she begins to tutor Baby, a member of a
ganglike non-conformist society called the Clan.
ISBN 0-688-16243-6
[1. Gangs—Fiction.   2. High schools—Fiction.   3. Schools—Fiction.]
I. Title.   PZ7.R1585Br 1999   [Fic]—dc21   98-27867   CIP AC

For Rosemary,
who is my friend,
and
for Alan,
who is *her* friend . . .
with acorns and clothespins
firmly in mind.

one

IT WASN'T THE MYSTERY THAT finally pulled Casey in, though curiosity could have been enough—if living with the shadow of the Clan hadn't been so much like having a time bomb planted in the middle of the kitchen.

It wasn't romance, either—for Casey, who was a nice girl, there shouldn't have been anything remotely romantic about the Clan. To the levelheaded folk in her little northern town, the Clan was decidedly strange, which made it seem just as decidedly threatening. No matter how quiet the Clan remained, decent people called it "lurking," and they kept half an eye there, just in case.

No, for Casey, it was—at least in the beginning—purely a matter of doing the right thing.

Over the years, several agencies had tried to deal with the Clan, but the Clan made no deals. It stood apart, like an odd, fervent religion, and held its own against everything. The few Clan in the community at large kept to themselves but did their jobs with uncommon competence. All of the members were young—most school age—and exclusively male, with no racial distinction. The common denominator seemed to be area of town, which could have meant geographical location or income level or both.

Whatever else the members might have had in common, there was a definite behavioral code that seemed to bind them all together. The most obvious thing was that they all wore black, except for bracelets of intricately braided threads—mostly black, but with one color or another shot through the black in what was evidently a deliberate pattern. The hair varied, but the distinct Clan mark was the tiny bead-tipped braid they always wore at the left temple, another pattern of deliberate color.

The schools had tried to address this, hoping to break up a social aberration by enforcing dress codes, but the Clan serenely ignored any such efforts. The schools had then threatened expulsion, but expulsion didn't bother the Clan, nor did threat of parent conferences or failing grades or, really, anything else; it didn't seem the school could take anything away from the Clan that it cared about losing. Certainly the young Clan were in school, obeying the law; no one could call them truant.

Perhaps the most disturbing thing about them was their silence. The young ones never spoke on school grounds. Never laughed. Never mocked, even with their eyes. Never even threatened. It was rare to see them talking, even among themselves in other places—though, in the course of business, the older ones seemed articulate enough when they needed to be.

As uncomfortable as its presence made people, no real action had ever been taken against the Clan, simply because the Clan had never done anything that could justify real action. Its members weren't openly violent or destructive or antilaw; they simply existed. And maybe that was what scared people the most—waiting to see what the Clan would finally *do*. But for twelve years, the Clan had done nothing. Literally nothing. The remedial classes were rife with Clan because their grades were a resounding baseline; no one in the Clan ever lifted a pencil in class except to draw pictures that no teacher got to see. No Clan member answered questions. Not one of them ever opened a book. The Clan just sat. Hour after hour. It nearly drove the teachers out of their minds. Every year, a new teacher would come in, fresh out of college and ready; halfway through the year, he'd be looking for a transfer.

And through all the twelve years of its existence, there was no known record of any *normal* kid having shared so much as eye contact with a Clan member. Never a conversation, certainly never a relationship of any kind.

Which is why, when Mr. Hall, head counselor at Feynman High, unveiled his Great Idea right in the middle of Casey's living room, Casey's parents were utterly dumbfounded.

Casey's mother gasped. "You're not serious."

But he was. "Just let me tell you about Thomas Fairbairn," he said, holding up one hand and scooting out to the edge of his chair. And then he explained the trap he had laid during testing, isolating each of the Clan carefully in a crowd of other students, hoping, he said, that if none of the other Clan could see, one of them just might get the courage to take the tests. And sure enough, one had. Now Mr. Hall trotted out those test scores—which were more than a little impressive.

"Which is why," he went on quickly, "we need Casey. If we're ever going to have a prayer of integrating this kid, we're going to need a mentor, somebody who's bright enough and aggressive enough to stay ahead of him, somebody the kids like—who can grease the wheels on the social thing. Casey's the natural choice—she's kind, she's open, she communicates clearly—and she's got a good bite of her own."

All of which sent Casey sliding down into her chair, rolling her eyes. Not that she hated hearing it—just that she was embarrassed about *liking* to hear it.

The talk flowed on around her, Mr. Hall pleading, her parents digging in their heels good and hard. "What about character?" her mother demanded. "Do you know *anything* about his character?"

"I know that his mother is a very good woman," Mr. Hall offered, "and that she'd do whatever it takes to pull her kid out of this mess."

Which brought everything to an awkward pause. After that, it was a matter of concessions—Mr. Hall assuring them it would *only* be a few hours after school, *only* on school grounds, *only* with supervision. Nobody would give out Casey's address or phone number. It would all be very cut-and-dried.

"You know it's not going to be that simple" was Casey's mother's answer. But in the end, "Shouldn't it be hers to say?" her father asked. And then they were all looking at Casey.

Who, in truth, thought the whole idea was very interesting.

"Well," Casey said finally, "didn't you always teach me I should help people when I can?" And that was pretty much that.

"There is a chance he won't want her," Mr. Hall pointed out as he pulled his coat on at the door.

"Yeah," Casey's mother said grimly. "There's always hope."

WHICH IS HOW Casey came to spend almost all of Friday's third period stuck in the corridor just outside Mr. Hall's office door—while on the other side of that door, which had been left slightly, and probably deliberately, ajar, Mr. Hall valiantly worked at exorcising Thomas Fairbairn's demons, eloquently extolling the beauties of education and painting lurid pictures of the hell he called "ignorance."

Of course, through it all, Thomas Fairbairn had not said one word.

At last, Mr. Hall fell silent—a silence that stretched into an almost audible tension, broken only by the sounds of someone shifting uncomfortably on a chrome and plastic chair.

"All right, Fairbairn," Mr. Hall said finally, winding up. "This is the proposal: We take you off your present schedule and put you in the honors program."

There was a gasp.

"It won't be easy for you. But it can't be as hard as staring at those cinder-block walls in Special Ed all day long. I don't understand how a mind like yours could stand the boredom." His chair protested—he was leaning into this. "I wouldn't be asking you to violate your silence if I didn't think you could pull it off—if I didn't believe this is what you wanted."

After a moment, Casey heard a surprised laugh. A distressed laugh, all air.

Another long silence. Casey kept expecting the door to fly open, for that kid in there to come stalking out.

"Honors." Another wisp of a laugh, bitter this time.

Mr. Hall asked cannily, "Why not show them what you can do?"

"Everybody who counts," the other voice came finally, "already knows what I can do."

After a moment, Mr. Hall said, "Do they?"

Out in the empty corridor, Casey pulled her shoulders together and grimaced.

"Here's the deal," Mr. Hall went on. "You make the grades, and I can guarantee you entrance into any state school."

Casey heard another sound, one that dripped skepticism. This boy shaped air so well, he didn't need words.

"And the financial aid is already in place." You could hear the satisfaction in Mr. Hall's voice.

"Look, Mr. Whatever"—the kid's voice was stiff—"the Clan doesn't believe in fairy godmothers. We never have."

Papers rustled—proof, handed across. And then it was quiet again.

"Signed by the Commissioner of Education," Mr. Hall declared. "No fairy godmothers, Fairbairn; nobody's giving you anything. Except a chance for you to get yourself something you want."

"And what would that be?" Thomas Fairbairn asked then—so softly, Casey could barely hear it.

"Your mother told me you're going to work for your brother," Mr. Hall countered. "So, that's going to be your life? Head under a hood and grease on your hands?"

"Partners," the kid snapped. "It's honorable work."

"True." Mr. Hall lowered his voice. "But is it what you *want*, Thomas?"

Casey checked her watch and then put her head back against the wall.

"You don't know what you're asking," the kid said. But he'd lost; even Casey could tell that.

"Why did you take the test?" Mr. Hall asked him.

"It was a mistake," Fairbairn said.

"You could lose your friends," Mr. Hall guessed.

"Family," Fairbairn amended bitterly.

"Your mother," Mr. Hall mused, "whom you would have to consider, I believe, to be family, was in here not a month ago, in tears because she didn't know what to do with you. She'd know all this if I could ever get hold of her. What do you think she'd be saying right about now?"

There was silence.

"People who love you want the best for you," Mr. Hall said quietly. "They're not going to choke you, or reshape you, or stand in your way when you want something good. People who do that—it's not love, Thomas." He paused, then went on, more gently. "So this is going to cost you. But I ask again—why did you take the test?"

A chair creaked.

"You want to think about it awhile?" Mr. Hall inquired.

After a moment, the boy said, wearily, "No."

"Are you saying," Mr. Hall asked slowly, "that you accept the proposal?"

There was a sigh, full of shards and splinters. And then, evidently, a nod.

"All right," Mr. Hall said carefully, obviously stuffing down a great surge of energy. "We start on Monday morning." Papers rustled. Casey stood away from the wall, heart quickening. Mr. Hall was coming—she'd heard his chair move. "Here's your schedule—the teachers will be expecting you. There's a seat marked for you on every one of these seating charts. You walk in; you sit down. We're not going to make a target out of you if we can help it."

"This is absurd," the kid said desperately.

"Mr. Belnap will tutor you in math an hour before school every day. And you'll have a daily peer-counselor session."

"Peer counselor," the kid echoed unhappily.

Mr. Hall came through the door. Casey felt a terrible jolt of nerves. Mr. Hall made a victory fist and reached for her arm, waving her past him into the room. She had a death grip on her books.

"Thomas Fairbairn," Mr. Hall said, behind her in the open doorway, "this is Casey Willardson."

Casey wasn't sure what she had expected. The kid was jammed into Mr. Hall's extra chair, one arm lying insolently along the edge of the desk, everything about him hard as marble. That much was no surprise. But the longish brown hair was clean and healthy-looking, and the black clothes were spotless. The little braided token at his wrist was an intricate weaving of black and yellow, and the tiny braid beside his left eye was tipped with black, green, and yellow beads. He glanced at her—eyes a startling medium blue, and face the color of humiliation; he knew she'd heard every word. He looked away the moment their eyes might have met.

"You and Casey have exactly the same schedule until lunch. Her job is to be your guide and your afternoon tutor, which means you put in an hour with her every afternoon, three-fifteen, in the library. She's good. Don't blow it." Mr. Hall looked down at his watch. "Now, I've got to do some things before lunch. If you want to wait in here until the bell, you won't have to worry about passes. Okay? Welcome aboard, Fairbairn."

He was gone before the boy could have answered—which he made no move to do. Casey stood there in the now-silent office, watching Thomas Fairbairn. He was messing with a paper clip, turning it over and over against the top of the desk. The color in his face hadn't gone down any. He wasn't going to look at her again. Not even the first time she spoke. Which she finally did, because the silence was too terrible: "I'll do everything I can to help you with this."

She got no answer.

Casey swallowed, her face stiffening. "Look," she said. "So you're scared." For that, she finally got a hot, hateful stare. "Fine," she said, forcing herself to meet those eyes. "So am I." He looked away, and the paper clip continued its endless circling.

She let slip a mirthless little laugh, shifting her weight. And then she waited.

"Scared of me," he said finally, all disdain. "It's not like I'm going to hurt you."

"Right," she said, and laughed again.

"What is that?" he demanded angrily. "You don't know me."

"You like to think so," she said, heating up.

"Oh, really," he retorted. "Going for stereotypes, are we?"

"Every time you're embarrassed," Casey guessed, "you're going to punish me for it. I can hear it in your voice. I can see it in your face, in the way you're sitting there. You're proud, and you're scared. And I'm the one who's going to suffer for it."

They glared at each other.

"Then why are you here?" he asked her, pronouncing it all very deliberately.

Her chin came up a little. "Because Mr. Hall seems to think you're worth helping."

"Oh," he said, dripping sarcasm. "Well. Thank you."

"Oh," she said, matching him tone for tone. "Well. You're welcome."

The bell rang.

"See you on Monday," she said, and she turned and left.

Halfway down the hall, she stopped. And then she turned and looked back at the door. He hadn't come out.

Somehow, it had gone wrong; the compassionate self she'd envisioned had disconcertingly come out Casey in Your Face. Not that he'd helped any. Reluctantly, she made her way back toward the door, steeling herself for the apology she was going to have to make. No sound came from the office. She eased the door open.

He was still in the chair, elbow on the desk, the fingers of one hand pressed against his forehead. His eyes were closed.

She lost her courage and fled, leaving him there alone.

SHE SAW HIM once more that day. Walking with Joanna on the way to fifth period, she passed him in the hall. Casey wondered how many other times she'd walked right past him without ever noticing. He was with some other Clan, all with their Clan faces carefully blank.

"Fairbairn," she said, and he looked up, almost startled out of "the face." She gave him a wry little nod. He made no answer, but he had seen her. Then he was gone.

"What was *that*?" Joanna asked her.

"The kid I told you about," Casey said. "My peer case."

"I don't care *who* it was," Joanna huffed. "You didn't tell me he was going to be *Clan*. Are you nuts? What was Mr. Hall thinking? You want to get yourself raped? You want people to think you're *asking* for it?"

"*Excuse* me?" Casey said, staring at her.

Joanna stared at her. "You know what I'm saying."

"I just said hello to him," Casey pointed out, offended. "It's just tutoring, my gosh. Everybody needs a chance, Joanna."

"Oh, right. A chance. For what? No, don't preach at me. Fine. Whatever. Do what you want—just don't let it carry over into the hall, because you're not going to like what happens if you do." Joanna waved a hand. "And you don't have to get huffy with me—all right—because I don't make the rules."

"Joanna," Casey said reasonably, "it'll be okay. Nobody's going to make a big deal out of it."

Joanna laughed. "And you really believe that." She rolled her eyes. "Of course you do; you always think there's going to be a happy ending to everything. You *know* that's a character flaw." She narrowed her eyes at Casey. "I bet you're feeling like some kind of angel of deliverance or something, huh?" She shook her head and blew through her teeth. "I can just feel it coming—this is *not* going to be good."

two

B A B Y   W A S   S C A R E D.
Somehow, it had never occurred to him that taking those tests could actually make anything happen. It had been curiosity, really. Maybe. For sure, it'd been a mistake. And nobody was going to like it—not the cribs, who'd already love to beat him to death just on general principle. Not the Clan. Nobody but his mother. There was going to be hell to pay.

And how in the name of heaven was he going to explain any of it to Lenny?

Because sooner or later, they were all going to find out.

Skyler nodded when he saw Baby come through the west door of the school into the fall afternoon. The sun was low, and Baby squinted against the bright flare of it. The rest of the young Clan, mostly blacks and purples and blues, were standing around on the lawn waiting for him, wanting to go home. When he started off across the faculty parking lot toward the field, the rest of them followed in a lazy wake.

"The Old Lady was on one today," somebody was murmuring. "What You Cannot Do or Be If You Do Not

Have an Education. She sounded like my mother's pastor."

All year, they'd been amused, watching this little college-girl teacher's earnest tries at getting to them. One day, she'd noticed somebody carefully sketching on what should have been a math paper; the next day, she'd introduced a "unit on art." String art. Coil pottery. Collages.

The Clan was easily bored.

And they were deeply amused at her assumptions: I know what you think you're pulling on me—but it's yourselves you're hurting. The truth was, she—along with everybody outside—knew nothing. Today, Baby had been scared to death of that ignorance, hoping she wouldn't slit his throat, letting something slip about those tests. But she hadn't even looked directly at him, not once. He had to be grateful to her for that.

He stepped up over the curb onto the playing field.

"We better wait for Monkey and Lance," somebody said.

Baby looked back over his shoulder and then turned around. "What's up?" he asked.

Skyler shrugged. "They do it all the time," he said. "We thought you knew."

Monkey had his head inside some teacher's car. As the rest of them waited, he pulled his head out and came trotting along, grinning, Lance at his heels. They'd left one of the doors of the car standing open.

"And that's not all they do," one of the aps said softly. "Hell, you can smell it on them all the time. I can't figure out why Shelly hasn't nailed them." Baby listened to this without turning his head. His face tightened.

"Let's go," Monkey said, panting.

"You want to tell me what you were doing?" Baby asked coldly.

"Getting a little change," Monkey said, grinning. He shook his fist back and forth, and they could hear coins jingle.

"Whose car was that?" Skyler asked. Lance shrugged.

"Let's go," Monkey said again, but Baby took hold of him.

"This is not our business," he said. "Shelly isn't going to like it."

"Shelly doesn't have to know," Monkey said, narrowing his eyes. He pulled his arm away from Baby's hand. The others were standing around them, listening. From the way Monkey was holding his shoulders, they all knew he was feeling their eyes on him.

"Are you Clan?" Baby said icily. "Because you get caught doing this, or you get caught toking up—yes, you know what I mean—you bring trouble on every one of us. Which we cannot afford. And I promise you, for that, Shelly will not be grateful. Nobody steals honor from the Clan, you understand? And this—you better put it back."

Monkey spat a word.

"Do it," Baby said. "And make sure the dome light goes off, Lance. Or you be here to push that car when it won't start."

"I'm not putting it back," Monkey said. A little murmur ran through the Clan.

"Then keep it," Baby told him quietly. "And be on your own."

The Clan shifted like disturbed shadows.

"Baby," Skyler murmured.

"You can't do that," Lance said, not sounding all that sure.

"He's Lenny's brother," Monkey sneered, not quite

meeting Baby's eyes. "He thinks he can do anything he wants."

"You step outside," Baby said, speaking quietly but hearing echoes in his head, "you stay outside. It won't go both ways. With us, or on your own. Ask Lenny. Ask Shell. I won't let you bring trouble on the Clan. You're not worth it, Monkey."

"It's just *change,* Baby," Lance said.

"It's just principle, Lance," Baby echoed. "Now, Monkey just remembered who that money belongs to," he went on softly. "He always meant to return it."

Monkey hissed, turned on his heel, and stalked back to the car.

"Go with him and make sure the door gets closed," Baby said to Lance.

"Sieg heil," Lance said, and trotted after Monkey. They all stood there, watching the west door of the school and willing the teachers to stay in the building. When Lance and Monkey had finished and were well away from the car, Baby turned around and headed off across the field toward town.

They had been boiling under their silence all day, but nobody felt like talking now. They were strung along in a loose orbit around Baby, sneaking looks at one another, waiting for the air to clear.

"They don't love you," Skyler murmured, tilting his head Monkey's way. The green and black beads of his braid beat softly against his cheek as he walked.

"I don't care," Baby said.

"Part of it's me," Skyler offered, troubled. "He feels like I got in his way."

Baby glanced at him. "When I took a green," he said

softly, "I never gave Monkey a thought. I never gave any-body else a thought."

Skyler nodded to himself. After a moment, he mur-mured, "Shell would never let Holt take Monkey. And Edmund won't take anybody after Tully, he said. Monkey's like a time bomb."

Baby laughed in spite of the acid in his stomach. "Shelly," he said. "Is that what Monkey's after? Why? He has no gift for the arts."

"It's the green," Skyler told him, looking at Baby oddly. "Don't you know that? It has nothing to do with gifts. Anyway, Holt doesn't have any art, either. Shelly should have taken you."

Baby looked at him again. "It's not my gift," he said.

"But you can see," Skyler told him. "And Shelly knows it. Everybody knows he should've taken you."

After a moment, Baby had to say, "I'm Lenny's." And Skyler nodded, because that was so.

It was a cold afternoon, the sun clear and thin, the light harsh above the yellowing grass of the field. A bunch of cribs came out of the field house, hands stuffed into the pockets of their letter jackets, headed for the school build-ing. As they passed the Clan, none of the Clan said any-thing. One of the cribs had a yellow-and-black Cliffs Notes hanging out of his back pocket. Kovacs saw it and pulled his face into what was supposed to be a Highly Intellectual Attitude.

"It's not that they're smart," Shelly always said. "It's just that they play the game. Crib notes, children—it's perfor-mance knowledge, not functional knowledge. The Clan doesn't play those games." Thinking about that, Baby's hands went clammy.

"So, where were *you* today?" Kovacs asked, as though

he'd just read Baby's mind. He was kind of skipping along sideways, looking at Baby. He was cheeky for as little blue as he had. "You were gone long enough. They send you to the office?"

"For good behavior," Monkey murmured, trailing along behind. Lance barely stifled a laugh.

Baby shrugged. For a second, he panicked—that Lenny should hear, that Lenny should ask the same thing before Baby was ready. But then again, why would Lenny think anything about it if he did hear? The office. Not exactly a rare trip for the Clan.

"You see that new girl they got in attendance in the afternoons?" somebody asked, swinging the conversation another way. "Very incredible details . . . "

Baby sighed and tried to unclench himself.

It was a long walk to the neighborhood. Too long, really, but the bus was too vulgar for the Clan, so they walked the distance every day, never mind the weather. The only cars belonged to people like Len and Shelly, people who had real money. And you counted yourself lucky if Lenny let you close enough to look at his car.

"What if you wanted to learn French?" Baby asked Skyler now. "How would you do that?" He was thinking too hard and missed the puzzlement on Skyler's face.

"Lenny reads German," Skyler offered. "So do you, a little."

"Because of the manuals," Baby said crossly. "It's not like we work on a lot of Peugeots. What if you wanted to *go* there? *That* kind of French—so you could speak it. You sit all day in that stupid schoolroom, and then ap the rest—how're you going to learn something like that?"

"Baby," Skyler whispered, taking a quick look over his shoulder. "What is it with you? You keep coming up with this stuff lately. You'd learn that the way you learn everything else. Get a book. Or find somebody French. What's bothering you?"

But Baby only grunted and lapsed back into his silence.

By the time they got to the neighborhood, their faces were stiff from the late-afternoon chill. Baby had been going on autopilot, caught in his own loop. Now he looked up and found himself lost. "Wait a minute," he said, stopping so abruptly somebody nearly plowed into him from behind. Baby looked at Skyler and opened his hands. "Why're we all going the same way?" he asked. "Don't we have ap sessions?"

Skyler had stopped with him and now was looking at Baby with something like fear. "Lenny had to work today," he said, but his voice was saying, How could you forget? "That's why we can't go to your house. Next week, he's got us nights on that BMW, but today we party. At Tully's house, remember? Baby, we been talking about this for a week."

Baby sucked in a breath. No Lenny. Not till dinner. Relief came cascading down the back of his neck, and his shoulders began to unknot themselves. "Fine," he said.

"But Tully's Marsh said Lenny's gonna finish early, so he's gonna be there after all. I thought Marsh told you. Baby? You okay?"

Too many hard shifts. Baby tried to focus on Skyler. "No," he said, because he wasn't quick enough to lie. Skyler stepped closer, making privacy. "What is it?" he asked.

Baby shook his head. "It's okay," he said, and made the effort to straighten himself up.

But how could Skyler buy that?

"It's just my stomach," Baby told him. "I don't feel so hot."

"Yeah," Skyler said softly. "I guess you don't. You want to go home?"

"No," Baby said, inside screaming *yes*. "No, it's okay."

"We gotta go home and get a book for you anyway," Skyler said, "Maybe you'll change your mind then."

"No," Baby said quickly, thinking about Lenny. "I don't need a book today." But he did. Oh, yes, he did. "Let's just go to Tully's."

"Fine," Skyler said, but he didn't mean it. He stood back and waited for Baby to lead off. They were all standing around waiting for Baby, wondering what was going on. So Baby headed toward Tully's, trying not to notice the troubled looks he was getting from Sky—and the murmuring from the rest.

The gatherings often happened at Lenny's house. It was the only place a member of the Clan actually owned, the only place the Clan was entirely at ease. The fact that Tully's mother worked full-time made Tully's house the second choice for a party; the mothers hated the music, hated the noise, and the few who stayed home from work had better things to do than mess with a house full of loud, lazy male people. But that's the worst it ever was, loud and lazy—the Clan always walked carefully, very aware of the eyes on them. So there were never any drugs, and no hard liquor, no disrespect to anybody, no trouble. The Clan always brought their own afternoon food because food cost money. And they always cleaned up after themselves because they couldn't afford to alienate the mothers.

Tully's house was like the rest of the neighborhood, a shabby square one-story box with a tiny forlorn front yard and a one-car garage in back. The young Clan could hear the music from the sidewalk, Shelly's jazz. Brecker Brothers. They all crowded together on the front walk, hungry and anxious to be home. They let Baby go first up the steps, courtesy of rank, pressing behind him. He put his hand on the doorknob, took a level, steady breath, and opened the door. The place was jammed.

Lenny looked up the second Baby worked his way inside.

"Baby Brother!" Edmund yelled, waving them in. "Hey!" Tully echoed. And then everybody was laughing and milling around, and the decibel level in the room rose to incredible heights. Baby sent a quick, carefully casual nod Lenny's way, feeling the lie all over his face. Lenny nodded back and then turned to say something to Edmund. Shelly was sitting over in the corner, sketching on a large pad, the detached look on his face meaning it was a job. And the rest of the older Clan, the ones with their afternoons free, lounged around wherever there was a place to settle.

Baby's bunch began to find their places, hovering around the food and then tucking themselves into whatever crevices were left, according to ap allegiance and caste. Edmund held up a bowl of pretzels; Baby crossed the room to take a few, hoping to settle his stomach. Edmund was the third white, one of the three oldest members of the Clan, and a gentler man than Lenny or Shelly; Edmund's personal space was always the safest place in the room for Baby. But Baby was too restless for safety and he drifted over toward Shelly instead, as far from Lenny as he could get.

The room was full of music and energy, a lot of laughing. Baby leaned against the wall just behind Shelly, getting a look at what was going down on the pad—a layout for a car ad. Shelly had sketched the car, and then a horse running behind it. The horse was powerfully drawn—a series of shapes and hatching, not really a horse, just shadows and spaces that made you feel the power of the animal. Shelly shifted, feeling Baby behind him. He didn't like it when people broke his concentration.

"It's good, Shell," Baby whispered, because it was, and Shelly looked up at him wryly, amused by the compliment. Baby felt his face go hot, pushed himself away from the wall, and went after another pretzel.

"You okay?" Edmund asked, looking up at him. "You look a little peaked."

"Fine," Baby said. More lies. "Tully," he asked, "you got some soda crackers?" Then he stood there alone in the middle of the room while Tully rummaged through the kitchen. A burst of laughter just behind Baby set him jumping.

Tully finally handed him a short roll of old Ritz, and Baby took it over to his usual resting place, the floor just behind and to the side of Lenny's chair. Baby settled himself there against the wall and reached for his book. It was a reflex. Now he was regretting his empty pocket. But Lenny didn't like it when Baby got lost in a book. Not on an afternoon like this, not when he thought Baby should be sociable instead. And Baby knew they all noticed when he withdrew, reading while the rest of them partied. He'd been right about the book; it was not a day for taking chances.

Holt was complaining about his carburetor. He had a junk heap of an old Camaro he was trying to rebuild, and there was always something he was trying to work out with it. Holt had no gift for engines.

Baby leaned back against the wall, finally beginning to

relax. He didn't mind sitting in this little backwater place of his, even though his view of things was more or less obscured by Lenny's shoulder. It was quiet by the wall, and he could watch faces without being too much noticed. Some of the faces he loved. Some he didn't mind. A few he had no use for at all. These people were the witnesses of his life, and where they were, he counted himself home, if not entirely safe.

"That's your problem, then," he heard himself telling Holt. "You can't do it that way."

"Why not?" Holt asked, pulling at his hair.

"Simple physics, Holt," Baby said, willing himself to stop.

Holt, whose right to wear the yellow nobody ever questioned, had years on Baby. He didn't like going down for his answers; it was Lenny he was asking. "I thought you told me that was exactly what I was *supposed* to do."

"No," Lenny said.

"So, what did you tell me, then?" Holt asked, sour and frustrated.

Lenny moved his hand, the white emblem around his wrist sliding down over the butt of his palm, indicating that Baby would explain. And so Baby did. Because Baby could. He knew a lot about cars. Baby knew a lot because Lenny knew everything there was to know about the dynamics of cars and engines; what Lenny knew came to Baby. And since it pleased Lenny to hear Baby shine, Baby shone as often as he could.

"So?" Holt said impatiently, throwing out the entire careful explanation with a gesture.

"So, it won't work, what you did," Baby said, unruffled. "You don't get it?"

"I'm getting it," Holt said, throwing himself back into

the sofa crossly. "I just spent a helluva lot of money *not* getting it."

Lenny looked back over his shoulder at Baby, sharing a wry smile. But Baby had a hard time with that, remembering his secrets the moment he met Lenny's eyes. He did his best to cover, scrambling to give Lenny back that smile, but by that time, Len had on a sharp, appraising look. When he turned away, his eyes said, You are one lousy liar. And when Baby saw that, the bottom went out of his stomach.

Right around then, the room began to center on Keele, who had been grinning to himself and humming over in his corner. It was when he winked at Holt that people began to notice.

"Don't look now," somebody said. "Looks like Keele's been gettin' a little."

"Which I most certainly have," Keele said, more self-satisfied than should have been legal. The talk about cars was definitely over. Baby reached unhappily for the book that still wasn't there.

"You going to tell us about it?" Holt asked, throwing a pillow at Keele. "Or you just going to sit over there grinning yourself to death?"

Don't tell us about it, Baby begged silently, one hand pressed over his stomach.

"Baby don't want to hear," Monkey said, leering at Baby from across the room. Baby immediately put his face into neutral.

"Baby never wants to hear," Holt said. "What's new?"

"What do you want to know?" Keele asked them, his voice suggesting that there was a lot he could tell.

"What do you think?" Lance giggled. "Start from the top." Stupid joke, but suddenly, the room was all attention. Edmund went out into the kitchen, and they could hear him rummaging around in the refrigerator.

Keele started to talk.

Please, please, Baby moaned inside himself. Not today.

Keele's experience was evidently fresh in his mind; he told about it with passionate eloquence. The way Keele talked about bodies, he might as well have brought the girl into the room so everybody could watch. Baby hated it. There was no love in the telling, no tenderness—just heat. And just now, Keele was still very hot. Baby knew that heat; he'd learned it listening to talk like this, and it was ugly to him. Whenever they started in this way, he felt a deep, brutal, personal shame, a kind of grief over the passing of something gentle and beautiful. What might have been left of Baby's comfort completely vaporized.

"I've got to go," Baby told Lenny.

Lenny sighed, didn't even turn to look at him.

"Really," Baby said, standing up. "It's my night for supper—"

"It's not that late," Lenny said, still not looking at him. But now everybody else was.

"Whatsa matter, Baby?" Holt asked, sounding bored. "We insulting your sensibilities again?"

"Don't you like the details, Baby?" Monkey asked. Then he made a vulgar joke that got half of them laughing their heads off.

"What's the problem with this kid, Lenny?" Holt asked, more or less teasing. "Baby Brother doesn't like girls? Come to think of it, how come I never see you with any girls, child?"

"He's okay," Len said.

"Just slow in his development," Holt suggested.

"Just sensitive," Edmund amended from the kitchen doorway, suddenly making it serious. "He'll be fine."

Then it was very quiet. They were all watching Baby. His face went to flame.

"How old are you now, Baby Brother?" Shelly asked quietly.

Baby looked at him but didn't answer. Lance was smirking.

"Look," Keele said, a man with a wonderful idea. "Baby's got a problem, right?"

"I don't have a problem," Baby said angrily.

"Oh, yes, you do, honey. You have an *attitude.*" Another ripple of laughter. "And it's time we faced it, don't you think?" He appealed to the room at large, and they cheerfully egged him on.

"Stay cool," Baby heard Lenny murmur. "You know they like to get you going. They don't mean anything, you know that."

"Well, old Keele has got the answer for you." Keele dropped another wink Holt's way. "I know this nice girl. *Very* nice"—he slid one eyebrow up—"and I happen to know she isn't doing anything this afternoon." There was a general murmur of dawning comprehension.

"What say we take Baby Brother over that way? And after he's done, we go out and he tells us *all* about it, and then we party till he drops? Bar mitzvah, eh? Good?" Scattered cheers and hilarity, mostly from the free Clan. Edmund's aps were silent, as were Lenny's. "What do you say, Baby? You could do worse your first time."

"And we'd all be with you." Holt grinned. "In case you get scared. We'll time you, even." They were choking themselves to death, laughing.

"Lenny," Baby said, very close to wanting to damage Holt.

Keele opened his hands, appealing to Baby.

"Knock it off, all right?" Baby said quietly, feeling humiliation on his face like fire.

"Look," Keele said, not smiling anymore. "I'm serious." And suddenly, he and Baby were glaring at each other across the room. The music had stopped.

"Sometimes you're too damn sanctimonious, Baby," Keele said. "The last couple of years, you sit over there looking at us like you don't want to get your hands dirty. It's disturbing. It's not natural, Len," he said, looking at Lenny. Somebody shifted weight, and the floor creaked.

"Isn't it about time you grew up, child?" Keele went on, his voice quiet. "Isn't it about time you joined the men around here and dropped this vestal virgin crap?"

Baby's jaw was so tight, it was beginning to hurt him.

"Listen, I make you an honest offer. This is a nice girl I'm talking about, Baby. Look at me"—Keele put both hands against his own chest—"I'm not kidding, now, okay? She's just like you—smart and quiet. You're not going to do better for a first time."

"He just sits there, judging everybody," Monkey said. "Like he's better than everybody."

It was very quiet in the room.

"I don't," Baby said.

Shelly shifted himself, cat-comfortable, casually weaving a coin back and forth through the fingers of his left hand. "So why don't you go with Keele?" His voice was so gentle.

Baby chilled.

"Leave him alone," Lenny said finally. "Any one of you guys want to stand up here and let the rest of us take a shot?"

"Hides behind his brother," Monkey murmured. They all heard him.

"You have something to say, Monkey?" Shelly asked, his eyes hooded. There was a flash of silver, and then his hand was empty.

Monkey stiffened. But he went ahead. "Some of us are sick of it," he said. "He walks around here like he thinks he's the crown prince of the Clan."

"If that's what Baby thinks," Edmund said quietly from the kitchen doorway, "he's right."

"Just because of Lenny," Monkey said. "Because he's Lenny's brother. He never has to stand on his own because of that. If it wasn't for Lenny," Monkey said, too far into it now to leave it alone, "you think he'd wear the yellow? You think he'd even be here?"

Now the room was absolutely still.

"If it wasn't for Lenny," Shelly said softly, "would any of you be here?" He blinked. "Baby Brother earns his place. I think we've had enough of this. Baby, if you've got to go home, go."

Baby swallowed. "I'll stay," he said. "I got a little time."

Shelly smiled his lazy half smile. "Fine," he said, settling back to his pad. "Keele, leave him alone. Somebody put on John Coltrane."

Somebody did and the music was loud in the room. Baby and Keele were still faced off. Keele finally shrugged. "Could have been nice," he mouthed, and turned away. Baby sank down in his place, heart still banging hard and hands shaking. For a moment, he felt smothered in that corner. A couple of minutes later, the rest of them were talking again like nothing had ever been wrong. Except that Baby had been perilously close to having no future. It left him cold; things could go bad so fast.

Lenny turned around and looked at him. Baby couldn't meet his eyes.

"Watch yourself, honey," Lenny murmured. "Watch yourself. That's all I can say."

three

EARLY MONDAY MORNING, CASEY TOOK A
long look at herself in the mirror. And what had Thomas
Fairbairn seen Friday in Mr. Hall's office of horrors? Not
a delivering angel, certainly. That nice little bit of self-
delusion had vaporized very neatly. Just a girl. A girl with
a snotty mouth.

She gathered a handful of blondish fuzz to one side of
her face and wove it back into a French braid, then did the
same on the other side. A green-eyed, nondescript, pride-
for-brains girl. And he was supposed to trust her.

But he was just as pride-for-brains as she was. Probably
dysfunctional. Definitely scared. Certainly belligerent. A
classic juvenile delinquent. Tough? Immoral? Amoral?
Something else? Something worth rescuing?

She threw on the little bit of makeup she had patience
for. I'm going to pull this off, she swore, chasing a smear
of mascara with wadded toilet tissue. I'm going to save
him—I don't care *what* it does to me.

She went into the kitchen and sat down to push her
breakfast around the plate, deafened by all the things her
mother was very clearly not saying. When her father

kissed her good-bye as he left for work, all he said was, "Think carefully."

Casey got to school early. But Thomas Fairbairn was there before her, the only kid in an echoingly empty homeroom—a black and brooding curiosity, midway back in the row of desks against the far wall. Casey hesitated then, sorry she'd eaten anything. Her hands were shaking.

"You're over there," Mrs. Thurman directed, indicating the seat across the aisle from Fairbairn's. Disconcertingly, Mrs. Thurman gave her a sympathetic look, mouthing, "Good luck."

And so it began.

Casey dropped her books onto her new desk. Thomas Fairbairn did not look up. "Hi," she said pointedly. Thomas glanced at her, nodded, and then turned away.

Shut down.

Okay, she thought. We knew this. We knew this would happen. She sat down, stowed her books, flipped open her notebook.

He was totally closed up behind walls of ice. She watched him out of the corner of her eye. His clothes were slightly different today—different kind of shirt, sleeves shoved up over his elbows, different cut of jeans—but still meticulously clean, and still black as the pit. And he still wore his face like a mask, carefully blank. The odd little braid hung just beside his eye, yellow beads loud against the darkness of his hair. He had a notebook open in front of him, but it could have been miles away, for all the notice he seemed to be giving it. Casey had no doubt that he was miserable.

"So," she said with studied indifference, "you went to Mr. Belnap's this morning?"

He turned his eyes on her. She chilled. "Yes," he

hissed. He held her eyes another three seconds, making himself very clear, and then released her. It wasn't a threat. Not exactly.

"You're a liar," she hissed back, answering those eyes, then turned her own face away. And, in doing so, she missed the small flicker of distress that slipped past the mask.

Out in the hall, lockers were slamming; noise levels began to swell. The door opened, letting in a rush of bright sound, and a kid came into the room. The door opened again. Two girls. The atmosphere around Thomas Fairbairn darkened and chilled another three degrees. The door opened again, and this time it stayed open, bouncing off the steady stream of kids as they came through. Every one of those kids took two steps into the room, saw the Clan, and did a double take. A couple of them looked around the room afterward, as if they were afraid that somehow they might have walked into the wrong one.

They stared at Thomas, and then they stared at Casey, because she was sitting next to him. After they sat down, they still stared. In four minutes, there was a whole classroom of silent, staring kids.

When Joanna finally came in, she hesitated, seeing Thomas. She glanced at Casey, swept a look around the room, and then found her desk and sat without a word.

Thomas hadn't seen any of this. Judging from the line of his jaw, seeing had not been necessary. Casey had an insane urge to move her desk closer to his; there was something very brittle about him, and the weight of the unwelcome in the room was pressing hard on her.

So, he had one friend. Whom he didn't want.

The bell rang.

The door opened once more, this time for the guys

coming in late from football practice. Big Gene Walenski was the first of them, laughing as he came in from the hall. Hair hanging down over one eye, he juggled his books and grinned straight at Casey; by this time, she was skewering everybody who came through the door with a ferocious glare that was hard to overlook. When he noticed Thomas, his face opened with surprise. The guys behind him had already taken the whole situation in, Clan and girl; one of them made a comment, and the group erupted in laughter as Walenski turned back to hear what had been said. When he looked across the room again, his eyes had narrowed.

"Gentlemen," Mrs. Thurman said, twisting the word just slightly. "If you don't mind?"

The knot at the door broke up, Casey's glare following the blue letter jackets as they scattered into their seats. Dickon Spencer was the last of them; too late to have caught the business, he happened to meet Casey's eyes as he slipped through the door. He flinched, not having expected that glare, and then he, too, saw Thomas. His eyebrows went up. He took a look around the room—which was still focused on the Clan—and then came back to Casey, face asking, What's this?

"Page fifty-nine," Mrs. Thurman directed. There was a lot of sudden thumping around, a settling of books. "So," Mrs. Thurman said, crossing the room to stand by the door, "when Cervantes says '. . . with little sleeping and much reading, his brains dried up . . . that he lost the use of his reason . . . ,' he is actually setting up the master irony that we will find later, driving the story. . . . "

She held the class tight for the next forty minutes, keeping relentless order and inspiring a desperation of scribbled notes. This was not business as usual. Casey had a hard time focusing. Finally, she stole a glance at Thomas, who had dropped the mask and was staring at Mrs. Thurman with a sort of helpless wonder. He had taken no notes.

When the bell rang, it startled everybody. Thomas blinked blankly down at the notebook on his desk. Then he closed it.

He glanced up at Casey, caught her watching. She looked away quickly, embarrassed. She heard a hollow sigh, and she was aware of him when he leaned over to pull the rest of his books out from under his seat.

Casey turned to him and put her hand on his arm as he straightened up. "Look," she whispered in a rush, trying to ignore the fact that it was her hand he was now looking at, not her face, "I'm sorry about Friday. I know I was rude— I never meant to be. I believe it's right to help when you can. I volunteered for this. I don't hate you. Don't hate me. I'm better than I acted."

He was still looking at her hand, so she removed it. "Please," she said. Two people sidled along between them, heading for the door.

Thomas looked at her. Directly. For the first time. "Thank you," he said. A kid jostled Thomas from behind, trying to get past, then suddenly changed his mind and went over-desk to the next aisle. This was not lost on Thomas. He dropped his eyes and turned to pick up his books.

"I can walk you to the next class," she offered, nervous about how he'd take it.

This time when he looked at her, she saw alarm in his eyes. "No," he said. Another sting. "Thank you. But . . ." He faltered, seeming to catch himself. He glanced over her shoulder and his face tightened slightly. She began to turn her own head, but then he touched her, put his hand on her arm, pulling her attention back. "Maybe you could do me a favor." Now his eyes were urgent and his voice was low and quick.

She nodded, trying to keep track of the changes and wondering what was going on behind her back.

"If you could just go on ahead and find the seats, so I don't have to stand in the doorway looking for them?"

"Sure," she said.

"If you could do that *now,*" he insisted.

"Okay," she said slowly. Then he smiled at her—just a tiny smile. She stood up, pulling her books together. "It's just down the hall a couple of doors and to the right," she told him.

But he'd already dismissed her.

She slung on her purse, picked up her books, and made her way to where Joanna was reeking of "So, you've got to tell me." "Come on," Casey said, ignoring Walenski as she passed him. She could see nothing out of the ordinary going on in the room—but her hands were still shaking.

"So, your Cinderella Man is actually here," Joanna said once they were out in the hall.

"More or less," Casey said tightly.

"Well, *you* seem thrilled," Joanna observed. "Look, I know I seemed real snotty about this before—but you gotta understand I'm seriously worried about you, Case. If you hear a rumor that they're forcing you to tutor this kid against your will, you can figure I started it. But it's obvious," she added hopefully, "you're having second thoughts, anyway."

Casey stared at her. "I'm not having second thoughts," she said.

Joanna sighed. "Of course not," she murmured. "Fine, you're doing a good thing—good old Casey, angel of mercy, what a surprise. Look, if you have to tutor him, you have to—except you don't *have* to—but okay, if you're determined to do this, then just keep in mind that if people think you're *hanging* with a guy like that, all of a sudden they think maybe you're not such a nice person after all. Or they'll think you're a little *too* nice, if you get me."

"What is going *on* here?" Casey said, still staring. "Why are you having such a problem with this? What was all that garbage going on when people came in this morning? I can't believe you guys are acting like this."

"Casey, he's *Clan*. Clan, if you haven't noticed, are not nice people. They're dangerous people. They don't want anything to do with us, and we don't want anything to do with them—I don't care *how* gorgeous they happen to be. That's reality, Casey; sooner or later, you're going to have to join in."

"And *that's* not insulting," Casey said.

"You could get hurt," Joanna pled.

"Oh," Casey said, "and you think *he's* the one who's going to hurt me? You know what's *hurting* me, Joanna? The fact that you could live your whole life with people, and then find out you were completely wrong about them the whole time. Yeah. Reality. You're right. Reality." She broke off, choking on the words. "See you around."

"Casey, come on," Joanna said, but Casey had taken off and was through the Chemistry Lab door before the words could have caught her. Joanna stopped dead in the hall, mouth open, until somebody behind shoved her through the door.

The next class was more of the same. It was a nightmare, and Mr. Schuller wasn't a good-enough teacher to figure out what was going on. So it never stopped. It just got worse—whispering, little knots of laughter. Fine, she sneered at them. I hope you fail the lab. But it wasn't like she'd gotten down a whole lot of notes herself.

Thomas was out of the door like a shot right after the bell, sitting silently at his desk in the next class before she could get halfway down the hall. They played leap-frog until lunch, when she lost track of him entirely. She didn't know if he'd made the classes he had without her. But she was fairly sure she wasn't ever going to see him again.

She was absolutely certain he wouldn't show up at the library.

But she was wrong about that.

He was there, all by himself at one of the tables stuck between the tall shelves in the back. The librarian pointed him out.

He was sitting—elbows on the table, head in his hands, flash of yellow at the wrist—with his books in a loose pile on the table in front of him, as though he'd just dropped them and let them fall.

He didn't move until she put her books down on the opposite side of the table. All he did then was glance at her and give a little nod. He looked worn. She pulled the strap of her purse off her shoulder and set the purse down on her books.

"So, how was it?" she asked him.

He looked up at her. "Exactly what I expected." He dropped his hands into his lap and sat back in the chair, not meeting her eyes. "This isn't going to work."

She pulled her chair out and sat down. "Nobody said it was going to be easy."

Then his eyes met hers, bitterly amused. "Really," he said.

Her face went hot.

"How is anybody supposed to process all this information?" he asked, disdainfully.

"It's not that hard, once you get used to it," she said.

"'Once you get used to it,'" he echoed, staring at her.

"You have me," she said with desperate patience. "So I can help you get up to speed."

"Up to speed?" he said. "Like all it's going to take is some kind of little adjustment or something?" He laughed, still staring. "Tell me you're not really this naive."

"It's just," she said a little breathlessly, "a matter of how you do things—taking notes, how you study." She blinked into that stare. And then she heard herself gushing, "You'll do fine. Don't worry about it."

His mouth fell open. And then he turned his face away, looking totally nonplussed. "What's-your-name, Willardson—"

"Casey," she told him stiffly.

"Whatever," he snapped, waving away the specifics. His eyes were hard and dark and held her. "I'm sure you're a very nice girl and all," he said, looking like he'd just picked up something vile, "but you're not listening." He put one hand carefully on the table between them and pronounced each word very clearly, in case she should be too stupid to understand: *"I cannot do this."* He held her eyes a second longer, and when he finally looked away, she felt like he'd dropped her on the floor.

"Okay," she said, breathing hard. "Okay," she said again. She stood up, a little light-headed, pushing the chair out behind her. "Well, then, I guess we should go tell Mr. Hall."

But he made an exasperated sound and opened his hands, like she'd said something totally asinine.

"All right," she said evenly, watching him. "If that's something you don't feel comfortable doing, I can do it alone. Or maybe you want to do it alone."

"No," he said.

She shifted her weight and heard her own exasperation slip out between her teeth. "I thought you said you didn't want to go through with this. Didn't you just say that? I thought you were just saying you couldn't do it."

He didn't answer for a moment. Then he shrugged. "I thought *you* were just saying I could."

She ran a hand through her hair. "Okay," she said, and she shifted again. "Look, I told you Friday I'd help you through this, and I meant it. But you're really making it hard. What is it you want from me? You're gonna have to tell me. You've got to come my way at least a little."

He was staring at her. He blinked a couple of times and then pressed his palms into his eyes. When he dropped his hands, he looked beaten.

She waited, but he didn't say anything.

"Just tell me what you want me to do," she said again.

He placed his hand palm-down on the table.

"Tell me I can do it," he said, softly.

So, why do you think I'm here? She shut her teeth on the words. He turned his eyes on her, and when she saw what was there, some wiser part of her right brain kicked in. He had no more mask. She sat back down on the edge of her chair.

"I believe you can do this," she said, as levelly as she could.

"Why?" he asked.

"Because," she told him, "Mr. Hall wouldn't have gone through all this for nothing."

"But why?" he said through his teeth. "Why? I don't understand *why.*"

"I don't *know,*" she snapped, her maturity worn through. "He's known a million kids; I guess he's entitled to his opinions."

He pulled back immediately, slamming the mask into place. But not before she'd seen what was in his eyes. *Reality.* And then she was scared. And she knew she was in way over her depth.

They sat there unhappily, the table between them.

"My parents always say," she said slowly, speaking around the pounding in her chest, "the thing you really want is the thing you end up with. So you look at what you've got, and you learn about yourself." She swallowed. "So, where are you? And what does it mean?" She paused. "Mr. Hall thinks you're gifted," she said. "So it's evidently not about what you *can* do. It's about what you want. The thing is"—she opened her hands—"what is it you want?"

He blinked. For a moment, she was afraid he wouldn't come her way at all. But then he said, "I want to go to college."

"Fine," she said. "For that, you need school."

"You don't," he said.

"Yes, you do," she said.

"Plenty of people get into college without graduating from high school," he said.

"No, they don't," she said.

"Yes, they do," he told her. "It's documented. You don't need school. You just need an education." Then quietly, "And money."

"Which you don't have," she concluded thoughtfully. "But which Mr. Hall does." He met her eyes guardedly.

"So," she said, and gave his books a little shove.

He regarded them hopelessly, hands against the edge of the table.

She folded her own squarely on the tabletop. "It's been a lousy day," she said gently.

One corner of his mouth came up.

"I'm sorry," she said. "I really didn't believe it would turn out like this. But you did, didn't you?"

He shrugged, nothing in his face.

"To hell with every one of them," she whispered.

He looked startled. And then he was studying her, as if he'd suddenly realized there was somebody behind that face. "You're actually kind of a hoyden, aren't you?" he said after a moment.

She blinked at him.

The other corner of his mouth came up. In spite of himself, he was smiling. More or less. "I mean that in the nicest possible way," he said, still with a mocking edge.

"I have no idea," she admitted—very reluctantly, "what that word means."

The smile turned into a disbelieving grin. "Well, then," he said. "Maybe there's some stuff I can teach you."

She laughed.

But she should have listened.

four

BABY'S HEAD POUNDED AS HE CLEARED
up the supper dishes. His books were stashed under his bed. It had taken an incredible amount of energy getting all those books home without any witnesses—crosstown bus to the downtown connection, then a long walk back up toward home, low profile on the back streets, skirting around Edmund's uncle's cleaners, wide berth around Royal's, all the time a nagging pain in his stomach.

Lenny had come home right on his heels, only staying long enough to get supper on the table. He had a vintage BMW on the rack, the kind of car Royal saved only for Lenny, his European specialist, and Len wouldn't let up till he'd taken it apart and fit it back together again, reveling in the play of the parts. It was the only thing he'd talked about at dinner. "Like a watch," he'd reported happily. "Beautiful technology . . . immaculate design . . . tell the aps they better have been through that manual. Warn them it'll be late every night this week."

He'd left again right after dinner, anxious to get into the work. Which meant Lenny hadn't seen anybody yet today, not long enough to know there were questions to be asked. Not long enough to hear that nobody had seen his little brother all day long.

Baby wearily rinsed off the plates. He was going to have to tell Len soon; nerves were beginning to eat holes right through his stomach. And the whole day's input kept going around and around in his head till he couldn't think a single coherent thought, let alone figure out how to approach a very complex thing like Lenny. All those years Baby had spent in remedial classes, frustrated and trapped and nearly insane with boredom—he was remembering them now with a kind of desperate nostalgia.

He could feel his mother watching his back. He hadn't eaten much. It was the kind of thing she'd notice. "The news is on in a minute," she said finally. The sudden sound of her voice made him jump.

"I don't think I'm going to watch tonight, Mom," he said, draining the dishwater out of a saucepan and trying to settle his nerves.

"You sure you can't come down with me?" Lenny had asked him, hand against the back door. "You'd like this car, Babe—it's art. If you want, I'll cancel the aps and we can do it together." Ordinarily, there'd have been no question. Ordinarily, there were few places he'd rather be than working with Len. They could have spent the whole night perched over the engine, tools going back and forth between them. Talking about someday, when they had their own place. He could have slept through school the next day.

But "I don't feel so good," he'd had to say, lying to his brother, hating to disappoint him. "My stomach— I'm just going to go to bed," he'd said, thinking about that pile of books, thinking about having to live through tomorrow. He'd nearly changed his mind, though, seeing the look on

Lenny's face. He was never a good liar, and now Lenny was a little bit hurt.

"Are you all right?" his mother asked from behind him. She wasn't used to this kind of silence with him.

"Sure," he said, and now he'd lied to everybody. "No," he corrected himself, having to tell her at least part of the truth. "I'm not. But it's no big thing. I think I'm just tired." He turned around and gave her a smile. Big mistake. It was a lousy, soulless smile, and she didn't buy it for a second.

"Maybe you ought to go to bed," she said, squinting at the kitchen clock.

"I've got some reading." He wiped his hands off on the dish towel and threaded it through the handle on the refrigerator.

"Why don't you come watch with me for a moment," she said. "I'm tired, too. But I hate to go to bed without spending a little time with you. Just for a while?"

He did the lousy smile again and nodded. His head felt heavy. Every part of him felt heavy.

"Come on," she said, and went into the living room to turn on the TV—Lenny's TV, a nice big-bucks box with seamless picture quality; Lenny didn't believe in depriving himself. "*The NewsHour*'s on," she said.

"I can't, Mom." He begged her with his eyes: Let me go for now. Just don't ask.

"Okay," she said gently, and folded herself into Lenny's recliner. Baby called Skyler, dodged his questions, and told him Lenny was going to keep the aps late. Then he tried to sit awhile with his mother, but he couldn't relax, and he didn't hear much of the news. He was watching his mother, worried that she looked too tired. And feeling guilty.

He liked his mother. She was a thinking woman, even

though she'd never finished school. She'd had Lenny before she was seventeen, and her family wouldn't have anything to do with her after that. But she'd never been afraid of work, even when it wore her nearly threadbare, and she'd done fairly well for herself in spite of everything. They hadn't had a house of their own until Lenny started making enough money to swing the mortgage, but now Lenny and his mother split the bills, and she had enough left over for a few luxuries—subscriptions to *National Geographic* and *Discover,* a small collection of esoteric CDs. She loved learning new things, connecting things; she was still young enough that she'd never quite given up the idea of getting more school.

"You get rich," she'd say, "and send me to college, all right? After *you* graduate."

She wasn't a beautiful woman. She was too tired, for one thing. And she never bothered to look at herself. But as he watched her face now, Baby thought he'd never seen anybody he liked better. He wondered if she'd ever get married again. Not much chance of it, working two jobs and not having a car. No time, no access. And she had ideas about that anyway: "I did it wrong once," she'd say, seeing in her mind two too-young kids, playing house for those five years she hardly ever talked about. "Next time, it'll be right, or there won't be a next time."

"Do you believe that?" she said to him now. She was arguing with something Jim Lehrer had just said.

He blinked. "I wasn't listening," he said. "What was it?"

She shook her head, and then she gave him one of those "I'm your mother, and whatever this is you're doing, I'm going to know it or die" looks.

"Really," he said. "I'm just tired."

"Uh-huh," she said dryly. When she turned back to the news, he could tell she was disturbed.

It was her right to know about him. But she'd go overboard, proud and excited, and then suddenly Lenny would know about it, and the Clan—and it was just too fragile a situation for that. But it was more than that; after everything she'd been through, he thought it would kill him to disappoint her now. And so his significant failures had to be private ones.

"I *gotta* go to bed," he told her. "My head is killing me." Another mistake. He saw alarm in her face. "It's just a headache," he said. "I'm not dying. And I'm not hungover or something, okay? Mom?" Please?

"Okay, Baby," she said.

He pushed himself up off the couch and smiled at her one last time, regretting it again the moment he saw her grimace in reply, and then headed for his room. He undressed, wondering how he could close his door without making her think he was sneaking around doing drugs or something. He turned off the overhead light and climbed into bed, then leaned way over, fishing under the bed for his American Systems book. He hid it under the sheet before he turned on his reading light and kept it under there while he read.

He'd meant to read his English, too, and finish his math. But his eyes closed all by themselves, and the next thing he knew, Lenny was banging around in the kitchen, probably making himself a little warm milk, and it was the dead of night. Baby lay there in the dark, a corner of his American Systems book sticking him in the ribs, thinking how he hated hiding things from Lenny, and wondering who had come in and turned off his reading light.

THE SECOND DAY wasn't any easier.

This girl guide of his kept surprising him. Obviously, she was thinking in far more sociable terms than he was. It made him unhappy, freezing her out the way he kept doing during class; she seemed like a nice-enough girl. But he didn't want crib buddies, and he didn't need complications just now.

Not that she was pressing him, because she wasn't. But the more patient she was with him, the guiltier he felt. That second afternoon, he'd expected her to break down and ask him where the heck he got off being so rude. But she didn't do it. She was a little guarded, like she was afraid he might bite. But she got right into the work, pulling him along with her, and pretty soon, he'd forgotten to remember she was a crib.

She seemed surprised about the things he knew—that he'd read some of the books he'd read, that he understood what had always seemed to him fairly basic concepts, as if she'd expected his life up to that point to have been empty; unaccountably, this had hurt him a little. Otherwise, she was a good tutor. Patiently, she'd explain the math in the physics, and then she'd start on the English. Nightmare stuff. Not the reading—it was the writing that was giving him fits.

"This is awful," she told him cheerfully about the first thing he'd written for her, and then she explained why. He felt utter despair—there were too many petty, incomprehensible details to keep track of. Commas. Topic sentences. "Just write the way you talk," she'd said—and when he'd done that, she'd told him how bad it was.

Then they'd checked the time.

"My mom's going to kill me," she announced, staring

at the wall clock, checking it against her watch. "I can't believe it got so late." She started packing up her things. "I swear, she'll be calling hospitals by the time I get home."

Baby had worries of his own in that regard. "I thought they closed this place before five or something," he said, slapping his stuff together.

"So did I," she said. She pulled her coat on. "It's completely dark out there." She squinted at the windows.

The librarian smiled and nodded and followed them to the library door with her keys.

"I'll walk you out," Baby decided.

"You don't have to," Casey said carelessly, as though she didn't know enough to be afraid of the dark. But he wasn't about to let her wander around in the night all by herself, so he followed her to the outside door and then held it open for her. She looked him over hard as they went out into the cold. No coat, he could hear her thinking.

"Let me drive you home," she offered.

"No," he said, standing there with that massive armload of books, thinking about this girl cruising his neighborhood after dark—about Lenny wanting to know who she was, and why she was carting Baby around. "Thank you."

He watched until she was safely away before he headed wearily homeward.

It was very late when he slipped in through his front door. He stowed the books in the coat closet, dropping an old jacket over them for safety's sake. When he finally got into the kitchen, Lenny, standing at the stove, turned around and gave him a hard, angry look.

"Sorry I'm so late, Len," he said, terrified by the look and wondering what it might mean.

Lenny turned back to the stove and jabbed at whatever it was he had in the pot. "It's not like you to be this late," Lenny said finally. "Not like you to cut school, either."

It had finally gotten back to him.

Len turned around and gave Baby a long, sober look. "You just better hope nobody says anything to your mother."

So, Lenny wasn't going to ask.

"Thanks," Baby said. And he backed out of the kitchen. He went over to the stereo and started going through the CDs, hands shaking. Beethoven's *Pathétique*. He slipped it into the machine and started it—ostensibly so that the music would be there for his mother when she walked through the door. The truth was, he'd chosen it for himself.

"Depressing," Lenny commented from the kitchen.

"It's quieting," Baby told him.

"You and her," Lenny said disgustedly. "By the way, you can bet she's not exactly going to be excited about this vegetable soup."

"Yeah. Well. Thanks," Baby said again. "Thanks for covering for me."

Lenny grunted. "Not much of a cover," he warned.

And of course, he was right. Their mother read the soup like it had big neon letters in it: BABY MISSED HIS NIGHT. She didn't say anything while they were sitting at the table, but she kept looking at Baby over her spoon. Lenny gave him a sideways look that said, Told you so, and she caught that, too.

Baby fed himself about half a bowl and then gave up completely.

"So," she said, talking to Lenny but watching Baby,

"what are you doing tonight? Maybe you and that nice Kate could see a movie."

Lenny stood up with his empty bowl and kissed her loudly on the forehead. "My dear Rowena," he said, "Kate was a year ago, and too high-maintenance—so give it up, please. I'm going out. You two can watch any boring little educational thing you want, and I won't be here to give you grief. Please—don't beg me to stay."

His mother slapped at him, saying, "Just because you have a problem with authority doesn't mean you have to be ignorant. It wouldn't hurt you to learn something about the world," but Lenny moved lightly out of the way.

"I know about the world." He laughed, and then turned a severe eye on Baby. "I believe you are on dishes?"

"I believe," their mother said, standing up, "the first thing I'm going to do this evening is go down to the church." Lenny handed Rowena's bowl to Baby, glaring down at him over it—a definite threat. "I'm late," Lenny warned.

"It wouldn't hurt you to go to church with me tonight, either," his mother remarked. "Just to let God know you're still around."

Lenny rolled his eyes and laughed again. His mother said nothing more, but her silence spoke tomes. "You're never gonna make a believer out of me, Ms. Rowena," he said, tweaking her under the chin. "You might as well give that up, too. 'I am the master of my fate: I am the captain of my soul.' And I wouldn't have it any other way."

"That's not Lenny I'm hearing," his mother muttered. "That's Shelly." The name came out almost a hiss.

"Actually," Lenny said, glowering at Baby, "it's William Henley. Baby?"

"I'll go," Baby told him, quieting the look. His mother

would walk to the old cathedral, three blocks west and one north, no matter how cold or dark it was, no matter who was cruising the streets. When she felt like she needed to go to church, she went—and if they wanted her safe, they went with her. Actually, Baby almost never minded. He liked the night, and he didn't mind the church. But just now, he was seeing hours of work time fading on him.

"Don't wait up," Lenny said, pulling on his jacket. Then he was out the door and gone.

"He could have dropped us off," Baby complained, taking his own bowl over to the counter.

"We like the walk," his mother reminded him, going for her coat.

"It's *freezing* out there," Baby called after her, pulling a piece of plastic wrap off the roll.

"Then maybe you'll wear a coat," she said. He covered his bowl and stuck it in the refrigerator; then he picked up the dirty saucepan and put it in the sink. She came back into the kitchen with his black jacket over her arm. "Leave it," she said. "I'll do it when we get home."

Obediently, he pulled on the coat and followed her out the front door, blowing little puffs of cloud into the night air as he waited for her to lock up. She came down the steps and laced her arm through his. They walked for a while without speaking.

"I was so young when I had Lenny," she said finally, the words an extension of some conversation she was having with herself. "I married the boy I was sure I loved and got out of my house." She shook her head. "An ignorant baby trying to raise a baby."

Baby patted her hand where it rested on his arm. "Put on your gloves," he ordered.

But she went on.

"I feel sad when I look at Lenny."

"Lenny's okay," Baby told her.

"He's not okay," she said. She sighed, and her breath came out in a cloud. "My life damaged him. Lenny's ideas about love are skewed. He doesn't care about anything but those cars of his and the women he sleeps with."

"*Mom,*" he said, shocked at her.

"Well, it's true," she said. "You think I'm stupid? I know more than you think I do."

Baby stiffened, and of course she felt it. She gave him a sideways glance. He fixed his mind on Lenny. It was Lenny she was talking about.

"He always pays the bills on time," Baby said, offering peace. "He bought us a house. He fixes faucets and windows. Mom, he's *always* there at dinner—I mean, he even cooks, right? He bought me everything I've got to wear. He didn't have to stay with us. Why would he do these things unless he cared about us?"

"He buys you clothes," she said coldly, "because he knows I won't buy you black."

Baby gritted his teeth. It was never good to talk to her about Lenny. Baby always managed to end up standing between the two of them. So he dumped the argument, jumping blind. "Actually, if I had a job, nobody would have to—"

She cut him off sharply. "Not while you're in school."

"I want you to *learn* when you're in school. Or, at least, that's what I'm always *hoping* for."

Another bad move. Another stock argument. And too close. Way too close.

"You know Lenny would do anything for you, Mom, if you asked him to. You know that. He loves you. I really think he does." Baby was so nervous now, trying to sidestep—he wasn't used to it, and the mistakes kept getting worse.

"Then you think wrong," she said.

"Well, he's good with me," Baby said, desperate.

"Yes," she agreed. "He's been good with you." She glanced up at him and then away. "A little too good," she murmured. She pulled her collar up around her ears. "Baby, believe me when I tell you, it's too late for Lenny and me. It was too late from the beginning. I love him, but my ignorance ruined him in a lot of very important ways. The only love he recognizes is pleasure. He has no sense of personal responsibility—the only person he's willing to sacrifice for is himself. And your father being the way he was didn't help any."

Baby stiffened up again. She blew a little cloud of vapor, patted him on the arm. "Baby," she said, "come on. You can't go on being scared to talk about your father."

"I'm not scared," he said. And he wasn't. It was just that, when people talked about fathers, it was Lenny's face he tended to see in his mind, kind of mixed up with Edmund's. What his mother didn't understand was how much it hurt Baby when she was so blind about Lenny, as though she didn't know him at all. And how weird it was for Baby to realize there'd been somebody else, somebody probably still alive somewhere, whose genetics, if nothing else, were all tied up with him.

"Doug wasn't a bad kid," she went on thoughtfully. "You have to understand that. He just wasn't strong. He didn't know how to *live*"—she made a fist—"how to farm the world. He always saw himself as a victim. He never could take hold and grow up. It was a very hard thing to live with. It was a horrible marriage. That's why I tell you, be careful where you invest yourself, because everything has a price. Doug and I didn't know that. And Doug never learned."

She looked up at Baby and smiled. "By the time you came along, I had finally learned a few things." She put her hand back on his arm. "I wanted you to have a beautiful life, Baby. I've tried to teach you good, solid values. I wanted to give you everything I love—music, science, ideas, faith. Everything that could make you happy. I tried to teach you how to be loving and respectful and honorable. Remember how I used to say all the time, 'Look at that person's face. How do you think he's feeling?' I wanted to make you aware of other people—how real they are. How important. So that you would never use people. So that you would be kind and honest. And I've been proud of you, Baby. Because it always seemed to me that you were learning."

So, he'd scared her—to make her talk like this, to make her feel like she had to remind him who he was.

"When you were very little," she went on a little dreamily, "I used to say, 'Baby, make me beautiful.' And you'd climb up in my lap and pat my cheeks with your fat little hands. You'd look into my eyes and smile and kiss me, and run your hands through my hair, all very seriously. 'Now you're beautiful,' you'd say. Like you'd really made it so."

He smiled into the dark. Somebody drove by in a car and leaned out the window to yell at him, just a greeting.

"Aren't you cold?" he asked, thinking she ought to have her hands in her pockets instead of keeping that maternal grip on him.

"I'm okay," she said, burying her chin in the collar of her coat. His ears were cold.

They went on another half a block in silence. A police car slid quietly by. A little biting wind came up. He could feel her listening, trying to work out what was wrong with him, and he ached to tell her what she wanted to know. But there was too much at stake, and his own emotional balance had become so delicate.

"I just wish I had more to give you," she said finally.

He was too tired for this. "Mama," he said, "you've done fine. What else could I want?"

"What else?" she echoed a little bitterly. "You live in Lenny's house. You watch Lenny's TV. You listen to every word Lenny says—heaven knows what he's taught you that I don't even know about. We need to get you out of there. You need a real home."

"I listen to you," he insisted. Now she was scaring him. "I learn from you all the time."

"Well, whatever it is I've actually succeeded in teaching you—just do us both a favor and don't throw it away." Her voice had gone husky. They stopped at the foot of the wide stone stair that led up to the door of the church.

He put his hand over hers. "I know," he said gently, "you're thinking I'm in some kind of trouble. I'm not. I know I've been acting weird. But I'm not in trouble. I swear to you. There are just things I can't talk about right now. I know you'll respect that, and I'm sorry to ask you to leave me alone about it. But that's really how it has to be right now. I'm not doing anything bad. I swear. Mama, you should know by now—I'd never dishonor you. Or myself. Mom, I'm trying really hard."

She was looking up at him, and he could see her face by the lights of the church door. She was even more worried now. "You have dark circles under your eyes like pits," she said.

He shrugged.

"Nothing illegal?" she asked him.

"Never," he said, looking her straight in the face—because he could about that.

"No girls?" she asked, giving him a very hard eye.

"No girls. No drugs. Nothing immoral. Nothing stupid—I hope it's not stupid." He smiled at her sadly. "I'll tell you when I can, okay? Don't worry. You got to remember—I'm not Lenny. I don't even drink beer."

He was hoping she'd laugh, but she didn't. He knew the look on her face when she reached up and tugged gently at his braid.

"You have the wrong idea about that," he said softly.

"No, I don't," she told him, and she turned and went up the steps and disappeared into the shadows of the stone doorway. He closed his eyes and sighed. Then he followed her, taking the steps slowly, his body still weighing very heavily on him. He put his hand against the chill roughness of the wall as he finally passed over the threshold, wondering as he always did what kind of tool could have cut that stone. Then he crossed the vestibule and stopped at the inner doorway, leaning against the rich wood of the doorjamb, peering out into the nave.

His mother was moving down the shadowed aisle toward the altar. The ceiling of the place soared above her, lost at last in dark obscurity somewhere overhead. It was a twilight place, and that suited Baby. He slipped in through the doorway and lost himself in the deep shadows that hung over the confessional screens. He put his hand out there, too, running it lightly over the carved wood. He had always been fascinated by the Gothic beauty of the church, the craftsmanship and the detail, but he always stayed in the back while he waited, hovering in the shadows.

His mother, having knelt at the rail, rose and went to the side, where tiny candles winked. He heard the distant, silvery sound of the coins she dropped and saw her reach to light one of the candles, knowing it was for him that she did it.

He closed his eyes, leaning back against the stony wall, hands in his pockets. For the moment, he cleared his mind of anything but the rough cold of the stone at his back, wondering how thick the wall was; he couldn't hear anything outside—no traffic, no voices. He sent his mind upward as though it were a hand running along the surface of the stone, up, over his head, past the little roofs of the confessionals, and then beyond the choir loft and farther, into the arches, until even his imagination could go no higher. It was black up there, and cold, and he wondered if his mother thought this was the place her God took when He came to listen. The stone began to hurt him where it jutted into his back, and that brought him back to where he stood.

The voices in his head were quieting. He was becoming still under the silence and age of the stone and the vastness of the church. The tension in his mind began to ease.

He thought about his mother's God, a God who needed a place like this, a house so big and old and dark. Some of the things she had said about Him made sense to Baby. Some of the things did not. He had his own ideas.

There was surely something in his own soul—a Presence most easily defined by its sometime absence. At times, it spoke inside him, using no words, but rising in joyous approval at the sight of light and beauty and order, until he was sure he had wanted these things himself all along. It had nudged him into taking the tests. Now it did not want him to quit. He could have chosen against it, but the emptiness that followed such a choice was terrible to him. There were times this Presence expanded inside of him until he wondered if he could die of the joy and the yearning. He suspected all this to have something, at least, to do with the God of this place. And when he followed his mother this far in, he often meant it as a gesture of acknowledgment and gratitude.

He knew Lenny would laugh at him for it. Not to be cruel. It was just that Lenny didn't like to depend on anything but himself.

Not so Baby. You hear me, he whispered in his soul, prodding at the Presence. You see what I've done. And now I'm in trouble, and I don't know what I'm going to do.

He opened his eyes and turned them to the altar. His mother was on her way back up the aisle, small and old-looking with the scarf over her head. Like pictures he'd seen of immigrants. Strangers in a strange land . . . He half-expected her eyes to have gone huge in a dark, gaunt face, but when she looked up and smiled at him, reaching to take off the scarf, it was just his young mother he saw.

"Let's go," she whispered, breezing past him out into the vestibule.

He pushed away from the wall with relief and followed her, his mind suddenly full of physics equations.

five

AFTER THREE DAYS, IT WAS OBVIOUS THAT
Mr. Hall had been vindicated: Thomas was bright. Just
how bright Thomas actually was had taken Casey completely by surprise.

Mr. Hall glowed over the daily reports she gave him,
reveling in the books that Thomas had read. Thomas evidently read newspapers also—his response to the civics
material was far from clueless. As a matter of fact, he had
definite political opinions, not all of them entirely comfortable for her. Mr. Hall also took great delight in this.

"And he's right," Mr. Hall confessed. "Plenty of people
have educated themselves without benefit of formal
schooling. Albert Einstein and Teddy Roosevelt immediately come to mind. The question is, What does that
observation indicate when it comes from the Clan?" Mr.
Hall wrote little clarifying notes all over her reports,
explaining that eventually he meant to write the whole
thing up as a scholarly paper.

Even with the physics, Thomas surprised her—he came
up with solid answers without any idea how he should
have arrived at them. But it was Art Principles and History

that floored her; terms like *Pythagorean harmonic ratios* didn't even seem to faze him. And when she, skeptical, had asked him for definitions, he—seeming mildly surprised at her attitude—had delivered. She took a little comfort in the fact that he couldn't spell *Pythagorean.*

And he couldn't write worth a darn. That's where he really needed her—paragraphing and commas and thesis statements. What he didn't seem to need her for was anything beyond the actual work. He said good morning; he met her at the library; he said good-bye. That was it. He wouldn't chat; he wouldn't walk with her; he disappeared at lunch. And she couldn't help but take it personally.

Her mother had come to her that second night, sitting on her bed in the dark, asking how things were going. Pausing to say, "The whole thing still scares me to death."

"It's nothing," Casey told her then, as she'd said before. "You've got to trust me, Mom. Don't you think you brought me up pretty well?"

"A little too well" had been her mother's odd answer. "It's just—Casey, you're so spoiled." And then, before Casey could protest, her mother had said, "Not by having things, although I suspect that's probably true, too." She'd put her hand out and touched Casey's hair. "I mean by love," she said, and delivered nothing after that but a sad parting pat.

The very next day, Casey started her own education. She'd lingered a little to talk to Mrs. Thurman about her research topic, just long enough to see Thomas Fairbairn running the gauntlet for the door—a hallway of blue-and-white letter jackets, of elbows and knees that found Thomas as he tried to keep his dignity in spite of them. Mrs. Thurman saw it, too, mouth tightened and eyes blazing. Casey followed them all out, grim with anger.

The boys trailed Thomas down the hall, making just-audible comments and killing themselves laughing.

"I tried to tell you," Joanna said, dropping in beside her.

Casey walked on, saying nothing.

Thomas disappeared into Mr. Schuller's class, the blue-and-white jackets crowding close behind him.

"So what do you think, Joanna?" Casey asked coldly. "What else can we do to punish him? You want to crucify him, too?"

Joanna stopped and stared at her.

"You think I'm like *them,* don't you?" Joanna asked, jerking her head toward Schuller's class.

"Aren't you?" Casey asked her. She pulled open the classroom door.

"I'm not cruel," Joanna said softly behind her.

Schuller gave Casey a cold "You're tardy," which she did not hear. She dropped into her seat, teeth clenched. She didn't bother to look at Thomas; he knew what she'd seen, and she wasn't going to give him the chance to freeze her out. But she caught a flicker of movement off to that side, as if he'd glanced her way.

"And so it follows . . . ," Schuller was saying. Casey flipped open her notebook and tried to fix herself on the lecture, but that scene in Mrs. Thurman's doorway kept replaying itself in her head.

When the bell rang, she rose with cold determination and waited for Thomas. Raising one eyebrow supercil-iously, he managed to acknowledge her presence and reject it, all at once. When she stubbornly held her ground, he silently gathered his books and got up to go. She followed him as far as the door, where she slipped in between Thomas and the waiting jackets.

"Can I borrow the notes from Schuller's class for last week?" Casey asked, manufacturing a smile for Gene Walenski, looking up at him through her eyelashes. He seemed surprised, but he said, "Sure," and was just beginning to return the smile when Thomas Fairbairn walked past him and out into the hall. Then Walenski's eyes narrowed and he looked down at her suspiciously. Still smiling at Gene, Casey followed Thomas out the door.

Thomas didn't say a word once they were clear. He stalked down the hall with his books under his arm, all ice and glower. *Fine,* she thought, and stalked right along beside him.

They turned the corner into B hall and nearly ran into a couple of Clan kids. In a moment of suspended motion, Casey saw the surprise—no, more like shock—in their eyes. They stared at Thomas. They stared at the books he carried. They stared at her. And then they were gone. Thomas sighed, almost a hiss—but he still didn't say a word. He stopped at the next class, stiffly holding the door for her. She passed him, crossed the room, and dropped her books on her desk. A moment later, he dropped his books on his desk. So they were furious with each other. And they were supposed to be on the same side.

After American Systems, she walked him to fourth period—maintaining silence—but she lost him after that. He ditched lunch again. And she was absolutely certain she'd never see him again.

But at 3:15, he was in the library, sitting in the usual place, a book open on the table in front of him, cheek against his hand. She stood there for a long time, glaring at him and wishing she had something to throw.

He glanced up finally—how could he not have felt the weight of that look? And then they were staring at each other, until she sniffed and walked the rest of the way to the table. She dropped her stuff hard on her side of it.

"Why didn't you tell me what was going on?" She was horrified to feel her eyes beginning to burn.

He leaned back in his chair, one hand on the pages of his open book, and took his time answering. "Just exactly what good would that have done?" he asked quietly.

She shifted and threw out one hand. "It's not like I'm not part of this."

He was still balancing in the chair, now studying her. "It's not like we're friends," he said.

She flinched. Then she took a little breath. "Fine." A bit unsteadily, she gathered her books back up. "See you around." She slung the purse over her shoulder and turned to go.

"Ho—wait," he said, and the legs of his chair hit the floor. "What are you doing?"

She stopped. "Going home," she said without turning.

There was a pause. "I thought we were going to work," he said.

Her chin came up a little. "You make up the rules," she said, still with her back to him, "fine. You want to play by yourself, fine—play by yourself. I have things to do."

She didn't move.

"You were just supposed to tutor me," he pointed out.

"True," she agreed bitterly, hating him, and she started walking.

"Willardson," he said, and she heard the chair shoot back when he stood.

She turned around. "He'll get you another tutor," she said.

They were staring at each other again.

"I don't want another tutor," he said.

She shifted her weight, her eyes on the bookshelves behind him.

He took in a deep breath and let it all out at once. And then he sat back down in his chair. She glanced at him surreptitiously. He was leaning with his elbows on the table, forehead in the palms of his hands.

Now she didn't know what to do.

He finally dropped his hands and sat back in the chair, looking at her, his eyes sore and shadowed. He glanced down and watched his hands open and close once, a helpless gesture.

"You look tired," she offered.

"Yeah," he allowed. "I'm kind of tired." He shrugged. "I'm not used to . . . ," he began, and then stopped. He swallowed and looked away. "I don't need a friend," he said. "I just need to survive this."

She pulled her shoulders up.

"This kind of thing, this social culling, has been going on," he went on softly, "since the beginning of the world. With people like them. People like me." He shrugged. "It doesn't bother me, Willardson. I wish you wouldn't let it bother you. And I wish you would sit down."

"My name is Casey." She did not sit. "Part of my job is to protect you from this kind of thing. And I intend to do my job."

Alarm showed in his eyes. "Leave it alone," he said.

"Look," she explained, "it's not as if these are evil people—I've known most of these guys all my life. Joanna and I used to hang out with Gene and Dickon all through junior high, and really right up through . . . right up until . . . ," but she found herself stuck there, and her face went warm.

"Until what?" he asked.

But her face had gone stiff. "Let's just say Gene Walenski owes me one," she said.

Thomas had gone very quiet. "No," he said. "Let's not just say that." She shifted her weight, not meeting his eyes.

"What happened?" he asked her.

"Nothing." She grimaced. "It was just a misunderstanding." He waited. "He just got a little out of line one time," she said, her face now hot. "He thought . . ." She lifted her shoulder. "He was just wrong is the point. It wasn't that big a deal. Except—"

"You're not friends anymore."

She shifted again. "It's not like we've been enemies," she said.

He studied the tabletop. "And the rest of them?" he asked.

"Just guys on the team," she said.

He nodded. And then he said quietly, "You know, it's very possible they would've gotten bored with me." He took a slow breath. "You could see that happening— sooner or later, guys like that, they've always got some other cat to hang." He looked up at her. "Unless it becomes a personal matter. Like, if you should get in the way. If you've done that, it's not likely your friend's going to let it drop. If he feels like his pride is taking some kind of shot, it could get very personal. And the rest of them'll go right along without ever giving it a thought. And if that's the way it is, I promise you, sooner or later they're going to need to hurt me. Or you. And then there'll be hell to pay, because I have friends, too."

His eyes held her perfectly still.

"So stay out of it," he whispered.

"Okay," she said, feeling oddly light-headed.

He broke the contact between them and she blinked,

moistening her lips. "But I still want to slap somebody," she said, narrowing her eyes.

He laughed. "You're a dangerous child," he said.

She came back to the table, muttering, "*He* says that to *me.*"

A little later, Mr. Hall stuck his head into their space, managing to startle both of them. "Well, guys," he said, frowning at his watch. "Everything okay here?"

"It's great," Casey said.

"And generally, things are going . . . ," Mr. Hall prompted.

Casey and Thomas shared a look. "Everything's fine," she said carefully. Of course Mrs. Thurman had told him about the stuff that had happened after class this morning.

"I promised your mom these sessions were only going to last an hour or so," Mr. Hall reminded her with a fairly transparent hardiness. "And Mrs. Shein"—he tipped his head toward the library desk—"has a life outside this room."

"We've been going a little late," Casey admitted.

Mr. Hall tapped his watch meaningfully.

"Maybe just another fifteen minutes," Thomas said. "I've got this paper—"

"Fifteen minutes?" Casey echoed, dripping skepticism.

"No later," Mr. Hall warned, beaming at them in spite of the words. "Or you're going to get me in trouble." Once he disappeared, they put him completely out of their minds.

"WE GOTTA GO." Casey glanced at her watch, and then stared at it, her mouth falling open.

Thomas sat up, stretched his back, and squinted toward the windows. Dark. He closed his eyes and stretched once more as she closed the books and put the papers in a nice little pile.

"Okay?" she said, and stood up.

He smiled at her. It was a nice smile—for once unguarded. "Thank you for staying," he said.

She shrugged, keeping her face neutral.

They left the library together and walked down the hall, footsteps loud in a silence she finally heard—a silence that seemed, in that place, a little weird. Casey looked back over her shoulder; the hallway behind them was shadowed and empty. Thomas backed into the door and it opened, spilling chilly air onto Casey's face.

"You're nuts to go without a coat," she told him, shivering inside hers. "You're going to be sick." He laughed. Maybe he didn't have one. Or maybe it just wasn't correct for people like him to wear coats.

They started off across the empty parking lot. Her car sat alone in the dim skirts of the streetlights. Casey squinted at her watch. "My mom said last night, if we're going to be late, we ought to work at my house. She thinks it's safer."

He didn't answer for a moment.

"We don't have to," she said.

"I don't think . . . ," he started, then hesitated, then said, "Let's not, okay? For now? If that's all right."

"Okay," she said slowly. "So, you don't want to come to my house?"

He laughed. "You're not real subtle, are you?"

"No. You're subtle. I'm accessible."

"I see," he said, smiling to himself.

"You're also avoiding the question." Her teeth were beginning to chatter.

"Okay," he said. "I can be accessible. No, I don't want to go to your house."

"Why not?" she asked him. "It's a nice house. You'd like my family."

"Uh-huh," he said. "I'm sure it's wonderful there."

They'd come to her car. She put her books down on the hood and opened her purse, fishing for keys. She found the keys, zipped her purse with maybe a little too much energy, and then looked him in the face.

"What is it?" she asked him. "You think we're rich or something? You think my parents are snobs? I don't get what your problem is."

"I think your parents," he said, "would rather not have me in their house."

"Didn't I say this was my mom's idea?" she pointed out. "Why would she suggest it if she didn't want you?"

"To keep an eye on things," he suggested. "Make sure you don't get into trouble."

She gave him a disgusted look. "Like I can't handle myself?"

"Willardson." The voice came from somewhere down by the shop building, loud enough to startle both of them. Now they could hear gravel under somebody's feet, and voices. Laughter.

Gene Walenski and two other guys strolled into the dim spill of the parking lot lights. They cruised across the lot toward the car, hands deep in the pockets of their blue-and-white jackets, streams of steamy breath trailing behind them. Casey took a quick look at Thomas. He met her eyes. "They were waiting for us," he warned. "You better go home." The way he said it made her chill.

"I don't think so," she said. But her stomach had gone cold.

"Get your books off the car," he said, putting his own down on the asphalt, "get in, lock the doors, and go home."

She picked up her books as he opened the car door for her. She put the books inside, but she didn't get in herself.

"Hey, Casey, what's going on?" Gene inquired, twelve feet away now. "You okay?"

Casey glared at Thomas, trying not to shiver. "Fine, thanks. We're fine. Everything's just fine."

"We heard you all the way over by the shop," Gene explained, talking to Casey but looking at Thomas. "Sounded like you were mad. We thought we'd better make sure nobody was messing with you."

"Go home, Casey," Thomas said. "You're gonna make your mother worry."

"Go home, Casey," Gene echoed. "Before you *catch* something."

"Gene," she said sharply. "Don't."

But he had moved closer, his friends behind him, grinning.

"Why don't *you* go home?" Gene said to Thomas.

"Get in the car, Casey," Thomas said.

"Why are you doing this?" she said to Gene. "You don't even know him." Something she didn't understand was happening here. Some kind of inertia, as if the asphalt was sinking under their feet, and they were all slowly falling toward each other.

"Get in the car, Casey," Gene said, his eyes on Thomas.

"I thought I knew you better than this," she said, voice

in her throat. She moved to stand between them.

Gene's eyes narrowed. "And I thought I knew *you* better than this," he said softly. "Or was I just missing out on something?" He reached for her, but Thomas caught his wrist before he ever made contact. Gene's friends stepped in from behind, and Gene seemed to catch fire.

"Don't touch her," Thomas said. Energy surged between Thomas and Gene.

"Hey, Baby." A new voice—soft, lazy—came from somewhere in the darkness behind them. Gene glanced back over his shoulder, searching for the source. It went on: "You have a problem?"

Casey leaned out around Gene, peering into the shadows. She heard Thomas suck in a breath. As she watched, there was a stirring in the darkness beyond the lights of the parking lot. Like bits of night taking form, the Clan melted out of the shadows; suddenly, they were standing where a moment before there had been nothing—a silent, insolent black half-moon, centered lazily, intently, on the car.

Thomas looked at Gene and dropped his wrist.

"It's all right," Thomas said, speaking into that silence. "These people were just leaving." His eyes were like flint chips when he looked at Gene. He said softly, "At least, I think maybe you should go."

"Later," Gene said quietly to Thomas, his own eyes hard; then he glanced over his shoulder once more at the black circle beyond. He didn't say another word. He and his friends turned around and sauntered away like there was nothing in the world they were afraid of. Like they hadn't just faced their own mortality.

"Will you go now?" Thomas said to her.

She was staring at the Clan. Staring at something that had formed itself out of darkness.

"It's just my brother, come to get me," he whispered. "It's all right now, Casey."

She pulled her eyes away from them and looked at him.

"It's all right, child" he said gently. "You're a brave little sucker." He moved her aside and opened the car door. "Maybe your mother's right," he said. "Maybe your house would be the best thing."

"Okay," she said as she moved into the seat. "Okay."

"Casey," he said, leaning over to look at her. She had both her hands on the wheel, but she hadn't put the key in yet.

"What?" she said. She was having a hard time focusing. She was thinking, This is what it feels like to be shocked.

"Everything's okay," he said. He reached into the car and patted her cheek. "It's just that Shelly loves dramatic entrances. See you tomorrow." He shut the door, and she put in the key and turned it, then turned on the headlights. He made a sign at her: Lock the doors. So she did. And then he stood there in the parking lot and watched as she drove away.

She didn't cry. Red eyes would be too hard to explain to her parents. They were going to know something was up, anyway; her face felt frozen, which was reasonable—the world outside had just become a colder place.

six

BABY WATCHED HER PULL AWAY,
watched until she was long gone down the shadowed
street. And then it all came on him at once, and his knees
gave way. He let himself sink till he was sitting on the
asphalt, his head in his hands. He didn't hear a sound out
of the Clan until they were all around him. Someone put
a gentle hand on his back—Edmund, probably. And somebody was asking, "You okay, Baby? They hurt you, man?"

He shook his head.

"They wanted to," he heard Monkey say. He looked up
and met Monkey's little smile. Just like you, Baby thought.

"You all right?" Lenny asked him, squatting on his
heels, his hand on Baby's shoulder.

"I'm just tired, Len," Baby said. "I'm tired to death."

Lenny was studying him. "Don't you think it's time we
talk?" he suggested quietly.

Baby took a deep, slow breath. "Yeah," he whispered.
"I guess we better."

"Get him up," Lenny directed, and half a dozen hands
did the work.

"I have the books," Edmund said.

"Come on," Lenny said, and he put an arm around Baby's shoulders. They left the light of the parking lot and started across the dark playing field. "So," Lenny said, "you want to tell us what's going on?"

Baby's mouth had gone dry. "I've just been going to school," he said.

"You lie," Monkey sneered.

"Truth," Skyler said. "We saw him there today. That's what we told Len." He looked at Baby. "When you weren't anywhere else around, we thought maybe you'd still be here. It's good we came to check it out."

"You want to explain?" Lenny asked. They stopped in the middle of the field, and the Clan made a loose circle around Baby, who was now shivering and hugging himself at the center.

"They changed my schedule," Baby said, casting around like crazy for the right way to do this.

"And that means?" his brother said.

"They gave me different classes."

"Who was the girl?" somebody asked.

"Yeah," Keele said. "Nice little set of wheels." There was a lot of agreement.

"She's not a girl," Baby said. "She's just a friend." They thought that was very funny.

"You never told us you had friends," Holt said, making it sound very physical, and some of them thought that was funny, too.

"She's just my tutor," Baby said, making it worse. They were enjoying this. "Look," Baby said, frustrated with them. "She's a good girl."

"Yeah," Keele said. "She looked like she'd be good. But, Baby—how in heaven's name would *you* know?"

"What classes?" Lenny asked. His voice was hard. "Why would you need a tutor?"

Baby swallowed, trying to moisten his throat. "Honors classes, actually."

The circle went silent.

"You lie," Monkey said again.

"It's the truth," Baby said.

"Uh-huh," Holt said.

"You asked me," Baby said, getting tired of it. "I told you."

"What would suddenly make them put you in honors classes?" Lenny asked, the ice in his voice pulling Baby back down again.

"They think I belong there," Baby said quietly.

Somebody laughed. Lenny did not. Baby hugged himself tighter. His teeth were beginning to chatter.

"And what would give them reason to think that?" Shelly asked softly from somewhere in the dark.

"Because when they tested us a couple of months ago, I did the test. Okay? I took it. And they saw the scores."

"Ah," Shelly breathed.

"Nobody takes those things," Monkey said.

"They do if they need to prove something to themselves," Edmund said.

"You're just determined to screw yourself over, aren't you?" Lenny said.

"Why was it so wrong?" Baby pleaded. "What's the point of letting them think we're stupid? They're not going to learn to give us any respect. . . ."

There was a murmur then, a soft hum of voices all around him.

"Teaching them is not our business, Baby Brother." The voice came out of the shadows.

Lenny turned on his heel and started off across the field toward the neighborhood. Edmund followed, catching up with him, some of their aps trailing along behind. Baby swallowed, watching Lenny go, and then he started walking after them. Nobody stopped him. They all followed along, but nobody walked close to Baby.

And then Holt, a little way ahead, smacked his hands together and chortled. "This is *perfect.*" He turned around so he was walking backward. "*This* girl," he said, like it was a revelation.

"What about her?" Keele asked.

Holt dropped back and put his arm around Baby. "*This* girl," he said again. "'A consummation devoutly to be wished.' Talk about unity of purpose."

"And that's supposed to mean what?" Baby asked, trying to shrug Holt's arm off.

"Don't you get it?" Holt asked him. "She's lovely—isn't she, guys? And you like her, right? You like her."

"Is there a point to this?" Baby hissed, but he was getting colder by the second.

"And she's a crib." Holt pinched his cheek. "Come on, Babe, consider the political resonance. I'm saying, *this* is the right girl. I'm saying, Baby Brother, I really think you ought to lay this girl."

"*What?*" Baby said, and stopped. Somebody ran into him from behind. The Clan came up all around him, their silence intense. He looked around for Lenny, but Lenny and Edmund were long gone.

"The consummate gesture," Holt announced with a flourish. "No violence; you should like that. It's an evening's pleasure for you. And it's literally saying to them—" Holt moved his hand up sharply, and the free Clan exploded with hilarity.

Baby was staring at Holt through the dark.

"What do you think?" Holt asked.

"Get out of my way," Baby said.

Holt let go of him. "Child," Holt said, all the lightness gone, "it's been a long time now you've been sitting on your little fence, looking down at us like you're not sure this is really where you belong. Maybe it's time you ask yourself—what are you gonna be, Babe?"

"I'm Clan," Baby whispered.

"Really," Holt said. "And how are we supposed to tell? By the way you're secretly playing the game over there?"

"That doesn't change anything," Baby said.

"But it does," Holt said. "Oh, yes, it does." He looked around the circle of listening Clan. "It makes us uncomfortable with you, Baby Brother—it fills us with doubt. Baby, Baby. We would be so much more comfortable if you'd just let us know, once and for all, which side you're actually going to come down on."

"What do you mean, 'which side'?" Baby said. "You talk like there's a war."

"Where've *you* been?" somebody said.

Baby fell silent, hugging himself. Shelly was standing in the darkness behind Holt, not saying a word. There was a tiny flash of silver coin in his shadow.

Baby swallowed. "You want to know what side I'm on, why don't you just ask me?"

"Man, you've been *showing* us," Monkey declared.

"Such a simple thing to ease our minds—a token, really," Holt went on, grinning. "Just meet us in the middle."

"In *her* middle," Monkey said, Lance snickering behind him. Something that had been carefully civilized broke loose inside Baby, but they caught him before he could get to Monkey. Monkey skittered away.

"Beating the hell out of Monkey—not bad as tokens go. But too easy for a little scrapper like you, Babe." Holt put a hand against Baby's chest and shoved him back a step.

"Okay," Baby said, breathing hard. "Fine. I'll give you your damn token. But choose something else, Holt. There's no honor in this."

Holt threw his head back and laughed. "Child, honor and sex have nothing to do with each other," he said.

"Give me something righteous," Baby begged. "I won't do this. It's not funny, Holt. Anything. I'll burn down the school, I don't care. I'll rebuild your whole damned car."

"So profane, Baby." Holt laughed. "No, I think we've found this child's trial." He grinned, shaking his head, a dance of dim highlights skittering across his face. "And I believe the Clan will speak it," he said, turning to the others.

"Don't," Baby gasped, grabbing at Holt's arm. But Holt shrugged him off easily.

"Does the Clan speak it?" Holt asked.

"Thus does the Clan speak," they intoned, and that was that, forever.

Holt slapped Baby's cheek gently and walked away. Baby threw one frantic look toward Shelly, and then yelled after Holt, stalling desperately, "I need time. I'll need some time if I'm going to do this right."

Holt laughed.

"Sure," Keele said. "Take all the time you want. Take a week." More laughter, flowing all around him as they passed, tugged along in Holt's wake.

"A week from when?" Baby asked doggedly. Holt turned around, laughing. "A week from Friday, how about that?"

"A week from Friday," Keele echoed, slipping his arm

around Baby's shoulders. "Trust me. You won't mind at all." Laughing, he punched Baby lightly just below the belt, and then he, too, was gone.

Shelly had been lingering silently in the darkness. Now he drifted lazily over and put his hand gently to Baby's ear. He moved the hand away again, shimmering silver. He pressed something into Baby's hand, flashed a smile, then turned and slid back into the others' shadows. Baby panted, watching until the Clan faded into a formless movement in the dark.

"What is it?" Skyler murmured, standing close, two aps at his back.

Baby started. He opened his hand. It held a silver dollar.

"Not everybody spoke," Skyler said quietly, stopping himself just shy of touching Baby. "It wasn't Tully or his aps. Or us. But it was Holt's. Shelly's. Which means nearly everybody else." He came closer. "Shelly scares me now," he whispered. "I don't think it's aps he's after."

Baby was looking down at his shaking hands and wondering what to do with that silver disk.

"I think he's watching us," one of the aps warned softly. "I swear he's standing right over there."

"I don't know," Skyler said unhappily. "But I think that's why he didn't go to Lenny and ask for you in the beginning. He wanted you to come to him." Skyler looked over his shoulder; he turned back to Baby and touched his arm. Then Skyler and the aps drifted away, following the others.

Baby watched until he couldn't see them anymore. He turned once, slowly, all the way around, but there was nowhere else to go. So he, too, walked into the dark, shoulders hunched against the chill, to follow them home.

"**LENNY.** *LENNY—PLEASE.* Len—" Baby followed his brother up the walk, the front steps, and almost caught the front door in his face. "Just listen. Please, can't you just listen?"

Lenny turned halfway around at the end of the hall and put a hand out, warding Baby off. "I said, don't talk to me," Lenny warned, and, pushing the living room door open, stalked into the light. Bach's *Brandenburg* Concerto came flooding out through the open door, drenching them with its joy. Their mother was sitting on the couch, a book in her lap—home and supperless. She looked up as they came in, peering over the tops of her glasses.

Baby was still standing in the hallway, his arms full of books, and Lenny was on his way out again, through the kitchen.

"Lenny, please," Baby shouted over the music, nearly exhausted. *"Please."*

"Leonard," Rowena called sharply. The sound of her voice brought Lenny up stiffly in the middle of the dark kitchen. She took off her glasses and laid them on the little table beside her, and then she got up to turn off the music. "Someone want to tell me what's going on?"

"Sure," Lenny said, eyes burning, coming back to the kitchen doorway. "Baby Brother is a liar."

"I didn't lie," Baby protested. "It's just I didn't tell you yet."

"Yet," Lenny spat.

"How could I have told you? I didn't know what was going to happen."

"Oh yeah, you knew. You sure as—" Lenny glanced at his mother, and the room rang with words he didn't say. "You knew for darn sure *this* was going to happen."

"Only if it got this far. I never thought it would go this

far. Lenny? Okay, I made a mistake. I should have told you about the tests right at the start, or I never should have taken them, but Lenny, you gotta—"

"Just what've I gotta do?" Lenny shouted. "It was a lie, Baby. You sneak around behind my back. You sell out everything we stand for. You sell out *cheap.* You make a fool out of me in front of the Clan. And now you want me to tell you it's just fine? Well, I can't do that."

"That's enough," Rowena said sharply. Both of her sons subsided, glaring at each other. She was standing by the stereo, a finger still holding the place in her book. "I want to know what's going on," she said.

Lenny was burning holes in Baby with his eyes. "Ask Baby Brother," Lenny told her. "You'll like it. You and him. I'll be out in the garage." He slammed his way out the back, tiny eddies of icy air swirling in his wake.

She stared after him, her mouth slightly open. Baby heaved a tremendous sigh and threw himself back against the hall wall, books heavy in his arms. "Damn," he said. "Damn it."

She closed her book and put it on the table beside the glasses, and then she sat back down in her corner of the couch. "You want to come in here?" she asked.

He pushed himself away from the wall. He dropped the books in a chair and himself onto the far end of the couch. She waited.

He rubbed at his eyes with both hands, fighting an irrational urge to grin.

He dropped his hands into his lap and sighed once more. "I took some tests at school," he said. "And they changed my program. I didn't tell Lenny about it."

She sat there, waiting. When he didn't say anything more, she asked, "That's it?"

"I didn't tell anybody," he said. "And now they're all mad at me."

"Changed your program how?"

Now he did smile, but not pleasantly. "It's honors, Mom. They put me in honors."

The silence changed. He looked at her. She blinked at him. "I don't understand," she said. "Am I supposed to think this is funny?"

"Yeah, it's funny," he spat, covering his eyes with one hand. "They put me in honors, and they gave me a tutor, and I didn't want to tell you because it's all so ludicrous. So that's why I've been tired. And why I've been so weird lately."

"They put you in honors?" she asked blankly.

"Yeah," he whispered.

"How can they do that? You don't even have a grade point average."

He shrugged. "They're the school," he said. "They do whatever they want."

"So, they put you in honors."

"Yeah."

She made a funny little sound and threw her hands up. "Well, that's wonderful." She started to grin, and she said it again, joy leaking out all over. "Well, that's wonderful, Baby." Now she was glowing.

"Yeah," he said dully.

The back door opened. Lenny thumped his way across the kitchen floor, jerked open a cabinet drawer and then slammed it. "He tell you what happened an hour ago?" he demanded, coming as far as the doorway. "You didn't tell her that? Don't you think you better tell her the whole thing? Or you still editing your life?"

"Lenny—," Rowena said, warning him.

"It's bad enough you won't let him work with me on Sunday, and you fill his head with mystical crap. You bring him up on your music and your books and your God and tell him the world is such a wonderful place," Lenny said, cutting her off. "So, when has this benevolent world been all that wonderful to you? You pump him up with hope for something you've never seen yourself. It isn't rational. It's fairy tales, Rowena. You confuse him. And you set him up. They're going to crucify him over at that school. That's what they *do.* They damn near did it tonight, and I can't always be there to make sure they don't. Nobody tolerates a second opinion, Babe—and that's what you are—and they're not going to rest until they make you disappear, one way or the other. What is it with you, Rowena? You're his mother. Why can't you be satisfied with what he *is?*"

Rowena's eyes flashed. "What exactly *is* he, Leonard?"

"Not like them," Lenny said, his voice low and passionate. "He's not bound by their rules."

"No," she agreed. "No. He's bound by *yours.* Your rules, where nobody but you wins."

"We win," Lenny said softly, "because we *see.* Because what we do has meaning. We win, Rowena, because we don't waste anything, and we take the time to do it right."

"Life is not a contest," his mother said.

"Oh, yes, it is," Lenny said. "There's only so much for anybody. And he can't have it both ways."

"And what exactly is it he can't have?" She rose, tightly angry. "He's the son of a stupid woman. He's the son of a stupid man and the brother of a one-dimensional man. We *chose,* Lenny. All of us. You surely did. You are what you decided to be. Don't put limits on him—there's a great big world out there, honey. Don't you tell me what *he* is. He'll be what he chooses to be, God help him. *You* chose. Now, you just get out of his way and let him do his own choosing."

"You're wrong," Lenny said, cold as ice. "I *know* him, and you're going to kill him."

"No," his mother said, straightening up to her full height. "You don't know him. You don't have a clue what he's about. You've had your chance with him. Look at him. And now it's my turn. Because I can help him find his way through this, and I'm going to help him—even if you can't. And that's what bothers you, isn't it? Because you can't. You can't go there."

He held up his hand, face pale with anger. "I'm out of here," he said. "I've done as much as anybody could do." He stabbed Baby with a look, and then he said, in a voice gone almost soft, "I thought you and me had our plans all settled." He held the look a second longer, then spun around and went out through the back, slamming the door behind him.

Their mother stood there, staring angrily into the dark of the kitchen. "He really thinks he can keep you in that garage the rest of your life."

Baby closed his eyes and pressed a hand hard over his stomach.

seven

"I DON'T THINK I WANT TO TAKE ANY MORE walks in the dark alone," Casey said. Five minutes to the first bell next morning, she dropped her books onto her desk. She was drooping a little. "I'm going to have nightmares the rest of my life."

So, she was making light of it. He was oddly pleased that she was still speaking to him. "I guess," he said, trying hard to follow suit, "you don't see much of that kind of thing on your side of town."

She smiled. "No," she said, slipping into her seat.

"We don't see much of it, either," he admitted. And then he smiled at her; it was another unsuccessful effort—he'd meant to look cooperative, encouraging, but he was just no good at manufactured cheerfulness. Especially not lately. At that moment, he smelled her for the first time—a clean smell, green and a little sharp, like trees, like spice, maybe. She leaned over to stow her books and her hair spilled down over her shoulder.

"I'm sorry," he said, deeply grateful that she didn't know the rest of the story—an odd reaction for somebody who'd spent a very bad night worrying about her; what he should do right now was go straight to Mr. Hall and get her released from the assignment.

She flipped the hair back over her shoulder and met his eyes. "It scared me," she confessed. A kid pushed between them, heading for the back.

"I know," he said. *It's still scaring me.*

A girl sidled by, talking to somebody in the next row over. Mrs. Thurman came in.

"You were right," Casey admitted. Her eyes were a strange green, with flecks of gold in the centers, like wet grass, shadowed. "I guess I'm going to have to start trusting you."

He did the smile again, feeling his stomach knot up.

The bell rang.

He took notes. It was getting easier; he'd learned to disengage himself and flow with Mrs. Thurman until her voice got that little edge to it—then he'd know she'd hit something she was going to remember saying, and so he should remember, too. It was almost a pleasure, like calibrating points or listening to music, because she was a smart lady, because she had a head full of interesting ideas, because she knew books he hadn't touched yet. But he still wasn't ready to put his hand up for her, to open his mouth in class.

When Gene Walenski and a couple of others came in late, Mrs. Thurman gave them a very public Sober Look. She didn't mark them tardy; she didn't even break the rhythm of her lecture. She did wander back to collect pink office passes off their desks.

When that happened, Baby glanced at Casey. Casey shrugged. When the bell finally rang, nobody got up to intercept the two of them. Nobody even looked at them.

"Well, well," Casey said after that, on the way down

the hall. "Maybe Gene's having nightmares, too." Baby shrugged. Someone got shoved into him on the off side, nearly pushing Baby into Casey. Interestingly, he found the proximity not at all unpleasant, so he stayed there, walking so close that his shoulder brushed hers, hoping to catch that green smell again. "So," she said, giving him an odd little look and moving away just a tad, "according to yesterday's discussion, we're not friends. Okay. We can be coworkers or something. Colleagues." She shrugged. "I can do that. If that's what you want."

"What I want," he murmured.

When the Clan kids came around the corner this time, nobody on either side was caught off guard. Until Skyler smiled and nodded and said, "Baby." Casey took three more steps, then stopped dead in the middle of the hall. Skyler and the others passed on, lapped once more in silence. "The Clan just spoke," she pointed out.

Baby had no answer. He forged on, suddenly sick. Casey caught up through a crosscurrent of kids and settled quietly in beside him again. A moment later, she looked at him, pulling up one shoulder and lifting an eyebrow sassily. "Well, is it?"

He blinked at her. "Is what?" he asked. People were watching them; *the Clan is speaking.*

"Is that the way you want it? Are we colleagues? Because that would be fine with me."

"You have to have a name for us?" he asked, unaccountably irritated. "Fine. Whatever. What happened to *friends?*"

"We're not," she reminded him. She looked at him and her eyes were laughing. "Isn't that what you said? I thought that's the way you wanted it."

"Why do we have to talk about this?" he complained,

trying not to notice the looks of people passing by.

"Why don't you ever answer questions?" she countered.

"I'm not used to them," he snapped. "And I don't understand why you have to define everything."

She nodded. And then she smiled. Not at him. To herself. And he found himself wondering just what that might mean.

WHEN THE BELL rang after fourth period, Casey took him by the arm, pinning him to his desk. "Come to lunch," she said. Her eyes flashed, as if she expected to have to fight for this.

"I have studying to do," he said. He was trying to ignore her hand.

"Studying?" she said, genuinely surprised.

"No," he said. "Really, I go out to the parking lot and smoke dope before fifth. Yes, studying. What did you think?"

But she wasn't going to say what she'd thought. "You need to eat," she told him self-righteously, giving his arm a sharp, patronizing little squeeze.

"And whose mother are you?" he asked, not quite offended enough to shake loose.

"Your welfare is my job," she reminded him primly. She let go of him and bent down to retrieve her books. "Besides," she said, hair hiding her face, "we should eat together." She sat up and shook the hair back, not looking at him. "It's good for the working relationship."

Then he laughed. The few kids left in the room looked

at him in near shock, but he couldn't help himself. "'The working relationship'?" he echoed.

She narrowed her eyes at him. "You're the worst," she said, and stood up. "Fine, do what you want." But she stayed there, waiting.

That's when he knew for sure he would go with her, even though the thought of eating in the midst of hostile strangers made his stomach knot up. "Whatever makes you happy," he said, capitulating. "But I hope you realize—it's going to be a very weird experience."

AND THAT IT did indeed turn out to be.

People stared; the Clan in the lunchroom was definitely a sociological anomaly. Conversations stopped when Thomas walked by. And started right back up again when it became evident that Casey was with him. Casey could feel the eyes, creepy little hits up her back.

"Told you," Thomas murmured, standing behind her in the lunch line.

She lifted a shoulder and grimaced back at him. He leaned across her and took a tray; then he handed it to her. She found herself smiling again, and she stalled around in the line, the space in front of her widening as the pressure from behind pushed him up against her back. "Go," he finally said, not unpleasantly, giving her a gentle shove.

She waited until he'd finished paying and then led the way to an empty table. He sat across from her. Everybody in the room was watching.

"I'm not sure I'm going to be able to chew this stuff,"

Casey complained, dismally sizing up the dry meaty slab squatting in the middle of her tray. "It's bad enough when nobody's looking at you." She glanced up, and a dozen eyes flashed away. But a lot of the people at the tables around were dropping back into their talk.

Thomas poked at his meat loaf and grinned. She lanced hers, smiling to herself. "What?" he asked, studying her, maybe trying to read her face.

"It's just you never do that," she said. He looked blank, and then held up the fork, making a question. "Smiling. Just smiling," she said. "I like it." In fact, she liked it very much.

He actually blushed. When he looked away from her, several dozen kids immediately averted their faces. And he shrugged, as if he were resigning himself to his fate. "Someday, they'll make you a saint for this," he said finally. "Saint Casey, patron of embarrassed but noble-hearted girls."

"I'm not Catholic," she said. "I don't think they could do that."

"Saint Casey," he amended, "patron of embarrassed, heathen, but noble-hearted girls. I'm not Catholic, either. Just related. But then, there's no danger of anybody making a saint out of me. Who's this?" His fork indicated a point over her shoulder.

"Hi," Joanna said, standing there with her tray in her hands.

"Hi," Casey said, her voice in neutral.

"So, do you two need to be alone? Or are you receiving company?"

Casey looked at Thomas.

"We're just talking," he said, with a strange little twist on the last word.

"Does that mean I can sit down?" Joanna asked, her eyes on Casey.

"Is this duty?" Casey asked her. "Or friendship?"

"I want to eat my lunch," Joanna said impatiently. "And I'm starting to get embarrassed, standing here."

"Then this is the place," Thomas said, pointing to a chair.

"Thank you, Mr. Fairbairn," Joanna said, casting a baleful eye on Casey.

"Oh, shut up," Casey said.

But of course, Joanna was not capable of shutting up, which was wonderful, because suddenly the world was full of talk and nobody but Joanna had to be responsible for it. She started in on something that her brother had done the night before, then covered everything up to the present moment, going faster than usual, maybe because she felt so ill at ease. Thomas sat there watching her, amazed and entertained, cheek against his hand. "Eat," Casey kept telling him. "You gotta eat."

"You're better than TV," he finally told Joanna.

"Thank you," she said to him, dimpling.

"Excuse me."

They all looked up. Dickon Spencer, on his way to dump his tray. Casey found herself pulling back from the jacket he was wearing. Dickon's dark face was stiff. "I just wanted to apologize," he said. The address was evidently meant to be general, but he was looking at Casey. "What happened last night was out of line, and I'm sorry it happened."

"You weren't there," Thomas said.

Dickon only glanced at him. "I apologize for my friends," he said, and left them.

"So what happened?" Joanna wondered. "Or shouldn't I ask?"

"Later," Casey said, exchanging a long, puzzled look with Thomas.

"It's you guys who are better than TV," Joanna said to them. "How can you stand all this controversy?"

And then Thomas smiled at Joanna. One of his real smiles.

"Friends for life," Joanna gulped, and she covered her face with her hands.

"HE IS ABSOLUTELY GORGEOUS," Joanna said later. "He has a great vocabulary—which is not exactly what you'd expect, considering—and he's nice and he's cute, and he is *abso*lutely gorgeous."

"He's interesting," Casey agreed.

"That's not what I said," Joanna pointed out.

"Joanna, it's not my job to look at him."

"So, you're telling me you don't have eyes?" Joanna sniffed. "Or is this denial? Because that's what it sounds like; I think you're attracted to him, but you're just afraid to admit it. And now this kid is coming over to your house every night?"

"Every afternoon," Casey corrected her patiently. "For a couple of hours. It's just a study session, okay, Joanna? I'm his tutor, remember? Peer counselor?"

"Uh-huh. Well, I'm just saying, I promise you, this could get to be a mess. You better watch yourself. Just remember I told you: You just really better watch yourself."

eight

BABY WAS GETTING ACCUSTOMED TO NAUSEA.
These days, everywhere he went, everything he did, he ended up feeling at least slightly sick. Riding in Casey's car, watching the neat lawns and wide-streeted neighborhoods flit by that first afternoon, he had to keep swallowing down the suggestion that she just take him back to school, drop him off, and forget the whole thing.

He was terrified of meeting her parents.

He already knew what they thought, just as he knew what his mother was afraid they were going to think, and he knew by now that Casey wouldn't suspect any of it. He'd gone over this meeting a hundred times last night in his dreams. He knew exactly how this nice middle-class mother was going to look at him. And he kept trying not to care.

"Are you okay?" Casey asked, glancing sideways. He straightened up, pulling himself together, wondering how transparent he actually was. "You're so quiet," she said.

"I was just looking," he said, truthfully enough. "I don't know this side of town very well."

She made a left turn and then a right. "It's nice out here," she said.

"Nice," he echoed, wondering how it felt to live under trees this big.

She turned again, went half a block, and pulled over. He bent his head to look up at her house. Not a large house—well, not huge. The yard was huge. Like a park. The house had a wide porch and a steep roof with a row of little shuttered windows poking out of it. It looked like a house in a TV commercial.

"Come on," she said, and got out of the car. He took a deep breath to steady his nerves and opened his own door. She'd started up the walk. He stumbled on the little steps that led up from the sidewalk.

"Come on," she said again, smiling at him but looking a little puzzled.

"Nice house," he said flatly.

"My dad and mom built it when they were first married." She led the way up the porch steps to the heavy front door. "They did a lot of the work themselves. My dad almost killed himself, falling off the roof." She put her books down on a little table in the front hall and shrugged off her coat.

"Is that you?" a voice called from somewhere upstairs.

"Hi, Mom," Casey yelled back, and was just opening her mouth to say more when her mother hollered, "Take the stuff out of the dryer, will you? And get the stuff out of the washer and start another load—"

"Mom...," Casey started, but her mother's voice dropped down on them from above, suddenly double in volume.

"Just *do* it! I've got the whole Relief Society board showing up at four-thirty...." The rest of what she said was muffled, and Baby could see the woman in his mind's eye, head buried in somebody's closet, clothes flying out over her shoulder.

Casey looked at him apologetically. She was maybe even a little embarrassed, and that comforted him a bit.

"I think she means it," he said.

"I better do it," she agreed. She hung her coat in the front closet and started to put a hand out for his, then remembered he didn't have one, and was again embarrassed.

"Why don't you just sit down and get started?" she said, pointing into the living room, and she started down the hall that ran back by the stairs into the house beyond.

"I could help you," he suggested, dumping his books beside hers. He had no intention of running into her mother alone.

"Forget it," she told him. But he followed her anyway. She went back through the kitchen—a large, open, warm-looking room with an incredible number of cabinets. Pots and baskets hung from grids above the stove and the sink. The counters were shiny red tile with gray grouting, and the wood of the cabinets was a sort of honey color. Baby liked the look of it, but found comfort in the stack of dirty dishes perched precariously on the counter beside the sink.

Casey disappeared through a door at the other end of the room, and when he followed her through it, he found himself in laundry-utility area, where there were an ironing board, a huge washer and dryer, a large industrial-looking sink, and mounds of unwashed clothes.

"Hello?" she said when she turned around and found him behind her.

"I said I was going to help." He ignored her look and patted the washer.

"Right," she said, smirking at him. "What do *you* know about laundry? Everything you've got is black." She pulled open the dryer and peered inside. He opened the washer and did the same.

"Not everything I have is black," he pointed out. "My underwear, for example, is white." They exchanged snotty looks, and he began to settle down inside. He reached into the washer and pried up a handful of damp clothes. "Move," he directed, his hands full of clothes. She still had her face in the dryer.

"Just a second. I wonder if she thinks I'm going to stand here and sort all this?"

"Move," he said again, heavy on the *v.*

"*Okay,*" she said, doing a mass excavation of the dryer by way of dumping everything into one large wicker basket. She straightened up and ran a hand through her hair, trying to keep it out of her eyes; what she ended up with was a full charge of static electricity, and tiny strands of her hair, like thin gold threads, were now standing straight out in a wonderful aura around her face. He laughed, realizing he kind of liked looking at her.

She pointed to the dryer, reminding him about his business. "Oh, yeah," he said, and he tossed the clothes in through the round opening. She started sifting through the dirty clothes that were heaped around her feet, making separate piles.

"That'll bleed," he warned her. "Better put it in with the darks."

"It will not," she said, a red shirt balled up in her hands.

"It will too," he told her. "I do my mother's laundry, okay?"

"This's been washed a million times," she said.

"Fine." He poked the tail of a towel into the dryer. "Do what you want."

"Fine," she said haughtily, and—after a second—dropped the shirt into the pile of darks. He smiled to himself, but she caught it and narrowed her eyes good-naturedly.

"Your family generates one heck of a mess," he said, nudging the darks pile with his foot.

"I guess I'm going to sort after all." She sighed. She dismantled a stack of baskets and started going through the clothes she'd just dumped out of the dryer. "Mine," she said, making a drop into one of the empty baskets. "Zack's." She held up a tiny T-shirt and squinted at it. Then she dug for the label. "I can never tell Zack's from Sammy's," she murmured.

"How many in your family?" he asked, watching her.

"Six," she said, dropping something that obviously belonged to her father in the basket just behind her. "Zack and Sammy are the youngest—three and seven. They'll probably drive us nuts this afternoon until they get used to you. They always fall in love with visitors. And then Peter, who is nearly fourteen and totally insane, and then me and Mom and Dad."

"Six," he echoed, wondering whether he should think that was a lot of people.

"How many in yours?" she asked him.

"Just me and Lenny. Leonard. He's twenty-two. And Mom."

"Just the three of you, huh?" she said, glancing up at him. "Must be quiet."

"Yeah," he said, pushing himself away from the dryer and getting back to work.

She reached into the basket again, but she paused as she touched the clothes, and when she straightened up, seemed to have forgotten what she held in her hands. She watched him as he leaned into the washer, and he felt her silence.

"What?" he asked, pawing up more damp clothes.

She shook herself, glanced down at the jeans she was holding, and then dropped them into a basket. "I was just thinking...," she said. She looked at him again, this time appraisingly.

"Let me put these in the dryer," he directed. She moved, leaning back against the big sink.

He could feel the question hovering between them, and a ghost of the nausea came back.

"How did you ever get mixed up with a gang?" she asked gently, almost apologetically. He glanced at her. Her face was serious. He paused, examining the question for underlying traps.

"The Clan," he said, putting the clothes into the dryer carefully, piece by piece, "isn't a gang." He shoved a wad of white cotton sheet through the round opening, then straightened up wearily, wiping his hands on his thighs. "We're not territorial. We don't steal. We don't vandalize. We don't carry weapons. We are . . . a culture. A society within and in spite of a larger society. Social iconoclasts."

He went back to the washer for the last handful of clothes.

"And do the rest of them talk like that?" she asked, smiling.

"English, you mean?" He straightened up, the last of the wet clothes in hand.

"'Iconoclasts,'" she said.

"Oh." He shrugged, knocking little bits of lint off the

clothes. He carried the clothes over to the dryer and began to feed them in.

"Am I out of line?" she asked with Casey-like direct-ness.

Yes, he thought. But then he looked at her and couldn't be offended. So he said carefully, "Why are you asking?" He couldn't keep an edge off the words.

"I'm just trying to understand you," she said. "But I should have kept my mouth shut, huh?" She leaned over and went back to the sorting.

He watched her for a moment, telling himself, There does come a time for reasonable dialogue. He shut the dryer door. "I'm so defensive?"

"You could say so," she agreed, dropping a tiny pair of jeans into a basket.

He leaned back against the dryer and studied her. "Not many people ask about the Clan without having some kind of private agenda. Dryer's full."

"I'll set it," she said, pushing the hair out of her face again. He stepped aside to make room for her, considering that it might not be so bad to be understood. And sud-denly it was, *Make me talk. Don't let me scare you away.*

"It's really none of my business." She hit a button with the palm of her hand and the dryer started. "I didn't bring you here to make you unhappy," she said, looking at him with those eyes of hers. She was being humble with him, but he knew by now how fast that could change. And real-ized how nice it was, knowing her that well. Just being there with her, like people.

He bent over and picked a couple of dark blue socks off the dirty pile. "Lenny, my brother," he began, dropping the socks on the darks, "and Shelly and Edmund"—a sweatshirt went on the colors—"started the Clan when they were, I don't know, nine, ten years old."

She kept sorting slowly into the baskets, listening.

"Lenny's a natural mechanic—he does all of Royal's classy stuff. Edmund was reading the *Wall Street Journal* and pretty much running one of his uncle's dry cleaners by the time he was twelve—now he runs the whole chain. Shelly's an artist; I mean, a real one, a graphic artist—he makes incredible money. There was never any question for them, what their lives were going to be; school didn't seem to offer them much, and it chewed up incredible amounts of their time. But the law said they couldn't quit, so they had to go. They felt like that was fundamentally wrong. And so they rejected it." He smiled at her, untangling two small, very dirty sweatshirts. "And that's how it started."

She nodded slowly.

"You want more," he guessed, starting a new pile with a white T-shirt. "Okay," he said. "Ask." Because he was finding that he didn't mind talking to her about it.

"Okay," she said thoughtfully, and then grimaced and snatched something out of his hand. "Oh, put that down. Don't mess with the whites, please." Coloring up a little, she dropped whatever it was onto the floor behind her. Then she shook out a small pair of pajamas and began to fold them. "What's that thing on your wrist?" she asked, not looking at him.

He liked what the blush had done to her face, and his fingers were tingling a little from the touch of whatever it was that she'd snatched. "Knowledge," he said. And then he realized he was staring at her.

"Knowledge," she echoed.

"Symbolic," he amended, giving himself a little shake. "Black is the absence of light. White is the presence of all colors of light. So it means that. Like a rank. New apprentices are black, and then you go up through the spectrum to white."

"Apprentices," she said doubtfully.

"I'm not doing this very well," he murmured. He poked absently around in the pile and pulled out another dark sock. "We have three masters—the ones that wear white, they're masters. Len and Shelly and Edmund. And they take apprentices. And then they teach them everything they know, and the apprentices go from level to level. Except, of course, everybody learns a little of everything. Lenny trains us in dynamic systems, Edmund aps business, but he teaches other things—literature, civics, stuff like that. And his yellow—his main instructor, Tully—he aps computers. Shelly does philosophy and everything else. He aps the arts. But he's in charge of the free Clan, too, the ones who haven't chosen yet."

She looked down at his wrist. "So, that's yellow, like . . . ?"

He glanced down at it. "Tully. Yeah. Main instructor."

"And that means . . . " She had a pile of things in her lap, but she'd forgotten them.

He shrugged. "I could probably take your car apart and put it back together so it'd still run," he said, feeling suddenly shy about it. "Well, it'd probably run a lot better, actually. I'm not like Lenny, though—it's just not my gift. But I do okay. And Skyler, my green, helps me with the actual supervision over the aps."

She took a deep breath and looked down into her lap. When she looked back at him, it was as if she was steeling herself for a slap. "I still don't understand," she said. "This sounds like a trade school or something. Which is, I mean, it's just not . . . what I expected from . . . "

He smiled a little bitterly. "I know," he said. "You think

we do drugs. You think we beat up people in dark alleys. You think we kill cats under the full moon." He pulled up a very long argyle sock.

"But you don't do those things," she said, studying him. He could feel the heat come up in his face.

"We don't break the law," he said to her. "We never have."

"You wear black," she pointed out. "You won't even talk to people."

"It's a moral stance," he said, and unearthed a pair of tiny overalls.

"Which means . . .," she insisted.

He stopped digging. "It's like . . ." He paused, considering. "You know that stuff Thoreau says in 'Civil Disobedience'?"

She looked at him blankly.

"'All men recognize the right . . . ,'" he prompted. But she was still clueless, so he finished it, "'. . . to resist . . . the government, when its tyranny or its inefficiency are great and unendurable'? You haven't read Thoreau?" He hadn't meant to sound quite so astonished.

"Excerpts from *Walden,* last year," she offered.

"Oh," he said. "Well, it's like all that. You can't just accept the status quo. You have to keep evolving—finding new ways, better ways, or your morality stalls out. Emerson says, '. . . whoso would be a man, must be a non-conformist.' It's like, the human spirit needs to keep asserting its independence, to keep growing. It has nothing to do with taking drugs. Taking drugs is like an evolutionary step backward."

"Emerson," she said.

"Ralph Waldo," he said. "'Self-Reliance.' Haven't you read that, either? Transcendentalists?"

"I know who they are," she said, going a little huffy on him.

"It's just that, the best way to learn is to find your gift and then go after it. Shelly hung around the museum, talking to art students until he found mentors. Now, he's both a student and a mentor—but not just of art, because when you study art, you study everything. Take harmonic ratios—the principle resonates through all knowledge, because it's actually science. And it has its metaphorical and cultural significance, too." He pulled at one small muddy denim pant leg, hunting for the other. "Same thing with Lenny. He hung around Royal's and read manuals and got his hands into everything until he was good; then he taught me. So, I read a little German. I understand physics, mathematics . . . and the honor in giving somebody your best work. And I teach the aps." Now Baby was trying to untangle the jeans from a pair of Dockers.

"You know," she said, "you're really kind of a surprise."

"Yeah?" he said, poking gingerly at a pile of mostly white things. "Well, lately, everything is a surprise to me. Anyway, I guess what I'm saying is, when you start learning, everything—numbers, law, history, politics, science, whatever—it all follows, because it's all part of this huge organic whole. But it starts with finding your gifts. Shelly says, 'To every man is given a gift . . . seek every good gift,' which is part of a long Mormon passage; Shelly worked the God out of it and kept the rest." He surveyed the pile of darks. "More than enough for a load," he decided.

"Take this, too," she said a little absently, tossing him an orange shirt. "So," she went on quietly, "do you believe in God?"

"The Clan doesn't," he said, working his hands in under the pile.

"Do you?" she asked.

He grinned at her. "I suspect I might." He stood up and dropped the clothes into the washer. "Do you?" He jabbed at the clothes, trying to work them down in past the agitator.

"Definitely," she said, thoughtfully peeling a sock off a nylon slip. "What about girls?"

"Do we believe in them, you mean?" He laughed. "You'll have to define your terms." He was looking around for the soap.

"Excuse me?"

"Girls: purpose and function of. A lot of us don't have much time for that."

"For what?" She had stopped folding clothes.

"For"—he opened his hands and made helpless circles with them—"girls. You know. Like, as in care and feeding of. Relationships, whatever. So, we mostly limit ourselves to recreation."

"So, that's the function of girls? Like pets or something? Like . . ." One eyebrow up. She was beginning to look dangerous. "There are no girls in the Clan?"

"*In?*" he asked blankly. Then he smirked. "Oh, I can see this—Lenny and Holt and female aps. I don't think so. So, after all my revelations, now you're going to go PC on me?"

"All these high ideals, but you still have this Neanderthal concept about women? And that doesn't strike you as contradictory?"

"It's not *my* concept," he said, offended. "And I happen to have a great deal of respect for my mother, who is about the only woman—"

A female voice said, "Fifteen minutes, and I've got the whole dang Relief Society—" Its owner—Casey's mother, of course—stopped dead at the doorway of the laundry room. She was an older version of Casey—golden-haired and gamine-faced—her eyes and mouth wide open at the moment. Obviously, she hadn't expected to find anybody in her laundry room but Casey.

Suddenly, Baby became aware of the fact that he was standing in the middle of somebody's dirty clothes, in one of the most private rooms of a private house.

Casey's mother blinked, then came to herself and closed her mouth. She smiled, but as she did, she looked Baby over, and in her eyes was the distaste he'd known he was going to see.

"Mom," Casey said, wiping her hands on her jeans, "this is Thomas Fairbairn. This is my mom."

He was badly off balance now. "I'm sorry," he said, opening his hands, indicating the piles on the floor. "I hope you don't mind?"

The guarded look began to dissipate. "You drag your friends in here and make them help you with the laundry?" She directed a half-kidding look at Casey.

"I made her let me help," Baby said.

"Well, thank you, Thomas," Casey's mother said with not unpleasant mock civility. "I forgot you were coming, or I wouldn't have been so unseemly. My life is a little insane these days."

"I thought you said you washed my soccer socks." Another voice, carrying through the kitchen. "But they're not—" And a face, popping up just over Casey's mother's shoulder. Peter, evidently, by the age. The boy did a double take when he saw Baby, his eyebrows shooting way up.

"So, what's going on here?" he asked juicily, the eyebrows working.

"Laundry," Casey said dryly. "It doesn't surprise me you didn't recognize it."

"I'll find your socks," their mother said, shrugging Peter's chin off her shoulder. "But, come to think of it, didn't I ask you to clean out the dryer this morning before breakfast?"

"So, who's this?" Peter said, pretty well fixed on point. "Like—you're Clan."

"This is Thomas," Casey said with resignation, and then, to Baby, "*This* is Peter. Mom, Peter got you again. Somebody did—you've got a clothespin on your collar, right under your hair. Other side." She smiled at Baby apologetically. "Family joke," she explained. "It goes on for weeks—Peter and Mom are the worst."

Casey's mother gingerly unclipped the wooden pin from her shirt, glaring at Peter, who was leaning against the door, chuckling.

"Don't you have something to do?" she asked him. "Like—your homework?"

"It's been there for ten minutes," Peter informed her, grinning. "I'm one up on you."

Mrs. Willardson exchanged a disgusted look with Casey, who was now checking her own person for pins. "Sorry," Mrs. Willardson said. "My children are very weird. You guys can work in the dining room—I'll put the women in the family room." She grimaced. "Be careful of my red shirt, Casey—that one under Peter's jeans. It bleeds. So, Thomas, just get one more load done before you go, okay?" She grinned at them and went back into the kitchen.

Baby and Casey looked at each other. Casey shrugged.

"You heard the lady," she said, and threw him another pair of dirty jeans.

THE REST OF THE AFTERNOON was work, punctuated by visitations of small boys who had fallen in love with Baby, and who proceeded to show him every possession they owned, one micromachine at a time. He'd examined each of these things soberly, until Casey, in a fit of distraction, finally banned them from the room. The house was full of cooking smells, and Baby was tired and hungry before Casey had pronounced his paper halfway readable; he didn't complain when Casey announced she would drive him home.

"However," he warned as she was pulling on her coat and digging for keys, "you may not want to drive me as often as I'm going to hope you offer."

She was laughing as she yelled back into the house, "I'm taking Thomas now. I'll be right back."

She let the door slam behind her and ran down the porch steps. "My dad's home," she said with sudden pleasure. "Gimme a second." She flitted across the lawn to the driveway, where her father had just lifted the hood of his car. He was leaning over the engine in his business suit, shoulders hunched up, trying to see by the dim outside lights of the house. Casey threw her arms around him, and he hugged her absently, staring glumly down into the innards of the car. Baby drifted over the grass toward them.

"What's the trouble?" he asked when he got close enough.

Casey's father shook his head and let out an exasperated hiss. "I don't know," he said. The man ran a hand through his sandy hair and looked defeated.

"He just got this car from my uncle," Casey explained.

"So typical," Mr. Willardson said. "I'm looking for something I can really depend on—you can't afford to worry about your car when you've got to drive into the city three days out of five." He took off his glasses—round lenses in thin, brown frames—pulled a handkerchief out of his pocket, and cleaned them. "And Mark tells me this is a great car."

"What does it do?" Baby asked, resting his books on the body.

"It's got no guts," Casey's father said. He put his glasses back on. "Give it gas and it chokes."

"Your uncle's local?" Baby asked her.

"No," her father answered. "Los Angeles. He had a kid drive it all the way here for me. I don't know, maybe the kid did something to it on the way up. I hate to think that, but I just—"

"No, it's okay," Baby said happily. "It's just the mixture."

"The what?" Mr. Willardson blinked.

"Air to fuel. Altitude. Here." Baby put his books down. "You got a screwdriver?"

"In the garage," Casey said. "I could bring the whole toolbox, if you want."

"Yeah," Baby said, and he pushed up his sleeves.

Twenty minutes later, the car was running smooth as silk.

"Simple problem," Baby told them, wiping his hands. "Miraculous cure, though, isn't it?" He was feeling very good.

"Absolutely," Mr. Willardson said, turning off the ignition. "How'd you learn that?"

"My brother's a mechanic," Baby said.

Casey's dad focused on him for the first time. "Wait," he said. "Royal's. Lenny."

Baby smiled.

Casey's father nodded, shutting the car door. "He dresses like you." He came around the front of the car as Baby pulled down the hood. "Royal calls him an 'artiste.'"

Baby warmed to that. "You ought to have him go over this thing for you. Then you wouldn't have to worry."

Casey's father grinned. "I could never afford him. Way out of my class." Then he stuck out his hand. "My thanks. By the way, I'm Chase Willardson. Chase."

"Thomas Fairbairn," Casey said, glancing at Baby a little apologetically as she tugged at the sleeve of his shirt. She waved her father toward the house. "I've got to get him home before Mom kills me," she explained. She shoveled Baby's books back into his arms and pulled him across the lawn.

"Big points with Dad," she said as she got into the car. "So, where're we going?"

In the end, he wouldn't tell her exactly where he lived. The idea of her driving around his neighborhood after dark, especially with things as they were, unnerved him. So he picked a neutral place—the Safeway on the main road outside the neighborhood. Close enough—the cold wouldn't kill him before he got home—well lit, busy.

She didn't like it, of course. "You don't have a coat," she reminded him as he got out of the car.

"That really bothers you, doesn't it?" he'd said, laughing at her. He crossed over to the sidewalk. "Lock your doors. See you tomorrow." He waited until she pulled away, and then began to thread his way through the cars in the lot, only beginning to feel the cold.

nine

BABY COULD ALMOST HAVE FORGOTTEN THAT HE was different.

It was Casey, of course—the way she never seemed to address the outside of him. And the fact that people didn't seem to be so surprised now, seeing him around the school.

That almost forgetting—it was not a good thing.

At Casey's house on Friday afternoon, he'd played with Zachary a few minutes before they'd started working, feeling almost at home. Casey's mother put a bowl of fruit and a plate of cookies on the table for them. All very nice. Comfortable. But then her mother lingered. And looking at the carefully cheerful face, he knew something was coming. She made a little small talk. Then she said his name— his formal name—pronouncing it with care.

"I don't want you to misunderstand me," she said slowly, obviously working very hard to be nonthreatening. "But I wonder if maybe from now on, when you come here, you could just, you know, wear something a little different, a little more . . . colorful." Here she paused, biting her bottom lip.

"I see," he said. He couldn't look at either of them. This had hurt more than he'd expected.

"Forget it," Casey's mother said quickly. "Forget I said anything."

"No," he said. "I understand." He closed the book and placed it on top of the rest. And then he stood up, hoping he could get out of the house before he had to face exactly how much it had hurt.

Casey stood up abruptly.

"Thank you for the help," he said to her, managing to keep his voice level.

The color had drained out of her mother's face. "Oh, Thomas," she said, sounding so sorry—and that hurt him, too. He picked up the books, and with half a nod, started for the door. He should have known Casey wouldn't just let him go. She caught him halfway across the living room and took hold of his arm; he couldn't shake her off without dropping the books.

"Just a minute," she said, her face flushed. She sent her mother a scathing glance, and then she turned to him. "One of the neighborhood watch called last night and chewed us out for having you here. He said now everybody was going to get robbed or something worse. My mother told him to take a long jump. So it wasn't like she meant—"

"We don't steal," he said doggedly.

"How's anybody supposed to know that?" She had a brutal grip on his arm. "People are scared of you. It's reality and you have to face it—whether it's fair or justified or not. It just is. And besides, can you tell me your brother and his friends didn't mean it to be this way? That they don't enjoy it that people are scared? 'In spite of a larger society.' So it's us and them, in our faces."

He moved, but she didn't let go.

"Am I wrong, Thomas? Tell me if I'm wrong."

He wouldn't answer.

"But you're not like that," she said, more quietly. And then whispered, "They scare me, Thomas. But you don't. You're too . . ." She shrugged, pleading with her eyes. "Most of the time, I don't even think of you as Clan."

"But I am," he cried, and then lowered his voice, conscious of Casey's mother watching them. "That's what I *am*," he said desperately. He was breathing hard. "I didn't do this to lose that."

She could have said, "Why did you, then?" and skewered him on his own contradictions. She could have said a million things that would have made it so much worse. Instead, she stopped, and the look in her eyes was almost more than he could bear.

"They're just clothes," she said gently.

"No," he said, quieter himself now. "They're not."

She was looking at him so directly, his head began to hurt. He closed his eyes. And she let go of him.

"I'm sorry," Casey's mother said, still sitting in the dining room, her voice a little husky. "Obviously, I don't understand your situation. But I never meant to make you feel unwelcome."

He needed to respond, but his face felt like it would never move again. And now that the passion had passed, he was feeling mortally stupid.

"Come back and work," Casey said. He opened his eyes. When she looked at him this time, he felt an odd vertigo, as though his sense of balance had left him completely. "Come on," she said, handling him with great gentleness. She tugged lightly at his sleeve. "Things just happen. Let it go. Let it go." Her eyes held him, and now he was falling into them.

Her mother stood up. "You can have the cookies anyway," she offered brightly, going over the top for his benefit. Casey's clear green eyes were begging. When she tugged again, he let her lead him back to the table.

AS THE AFTERNOON WORE ON, Thomas couldn't seem to focus on anything, and the truth was, neither could Casey. Something had happened between them. Something that had nothing to do with vectors or syntax. Whatever it was, Thomas couldn't write through it. He did try. He wrote three dogged, absolutely useless pages before Casey finally called it quits.

He was invited to dinner, but he explained that it was his night to make supper. This made huge points with Casey's mother, the more so because he seemed so mystified that she should be impressed.

In the car, all the way back to his side of town, he was silent.

"Let me drive you to your house tonight," Casey begged, coming up on the Safeway—offering partly because it was so cold, mostly because she had a hunger to see where he lived, where he came from. But he remained adamant.

She pulled all the way into the Safeway lot, into the darkest corner she could find, and parked, shutting down the engine. He had his books in his lap, his hand on the door handle. She reached out and touched his arm. He froze at the touch, eyes fixed on the windshield.

"What is it?" she asked, suddenly terrified. "You don't want to work with me anymore. Thomas, you're not going to quit? Because I don't want you to quit. Thomas. Tell me. What is it?"

But he didn't answer. He took a quick glance at her and then pulled the door handle. The door popped but didn't come open far enough to trigger the dome lights.

"Thomas," she whispered again, every nerve in her arms and her hands and her face ringing.

He closed his eyes. Then he opened them and leaned over, placing his books carefully, tenderly, on the floor of the car. He straightened up slowly. And then he turned to her. There were words in his eyes, but he didn't speak them. He took her face gently between his hands. And then he kissed her.

When he was finished, he pulled away—not far— and let go of her. His hands, shaking now, hovered only inches from her face. "This makes things so much more complicated," he whispered.

But she could only stare at him.

He made a helpless sound and then shook himself. Collected his books. Got out of the car. He leaned over, looking at her. "Tomorrow's Saturday," he said. "I still don't have a paper."

"You should come," she said, her voice anything but steady. "Tomorrow. To my house."

"Morning?" he asked. "Afternoon?"

Now.

"Afternoon," she said, finally getting her breath. He nodded.

"See you," he said. But he didn't smile. He backed into the dark and closed the door. The dome light went out. She touched the lock—a reflex—and felt every door in the car snug down tight. She looked for him as she pulled out of the lot, but by then he was gone.

BABY CAME SOFTLY IN through his front door, his head full of leaves and fireworks and moonbeams. If the night walk had been cold, he hadn't noticed it. He shut the door behind himself and stowed his books in the front closet, out of Lenny's sight.

"Hey," Skyler said as Baby came into the light at the end of the hall. "You almost missed us. We were just taking off." Baby froze in the doorway, hugging himself.

"You okay?" Skyler asked him.

"Baby," Edmund said, smiling at him. "Come on in here. You look frozen."

"How's it goin'?" Keele asked, smirking. Every face in the room turned on Baby. Baby said nothing. Keele grinned at him. "Gettin' any?"

But Baby had no answer to that. He just wasn't quick enough with the changes. And he was too transparent.

"He is," crowed Holt. Baby wouldn't look at him. Skyler stood up. Holt laughed. "He truly is," Holt declared. "Why don't you tell us all about it, child?"

Lenny was standing in the kitchen doorway, arms crossed, waiting. Baby couldn't look at him, either. His hands were shaking. He tried so hard to clear his face.

"About what?" Edmund asked, looking around like he must have missed something. Shelly was sitting in Lenny's recliner over in the corner, watching it all.

"Didn't anybody tell Edmund?" Keele asked, laughing.

"Tell me what?" Edmund asked, half-smiling until he happened to meet Baby's eyes. "What's going on?"

So they told him all about it. And the more hilarious they got, the starker Edmund's face became.

"Tell me you're not serious," he said finally.

"Totally serious," Keele said, eyes half-lidded, still grinning.

"You let them do this?" Edmund said to Shelly.

"Come on, Edmund," Holt said, slapping him on the back. "This is the best piece of business we've had going in months."

"Seems to me you'd be saying that about your work," Edmund said quietly. But Holt made a derisive sound and rolled his eyes. "Well, this is going to stop right now," Edmund said. "You can't let this go on."

"Sure we can," Holt told him.

"No," Edmund said. "You can't." It was finally getting through to them how serious he was. "This kid is not made like you. He can't take this kind of stunt. Shelly," he said calmly, "you need to deal with this."

But Shelly sat deep in the chair, the fingers of one hand steepled delicately across his lips. When he smiled, the fingers spread in a miniature shrug. Holt said, "The Clan spoke."

The room was quiet now. Neither Edmund nor Shelly moved, but the tension between them was humming.

"Who?" Edmund asked. "Who spoke?"

Shelly moved his hand out, palm up, meaning everyone in the room.

Edmund looked around at them, and most of them couldn't meet his eyes. When he came to Lenny, they shared a long, dark look.

"This is not the Clan," Edmund said at last, hand indicating the room, voice gone throaty and low with unaccustomed anger. "We were the Clan," he went on softly, holding up the wrist that wore the white. "*You,*" he said to Shelly, "are the Clan." He lowered his hand slowly. "This is not what we started, Shelly. Why aren't these boys working? Tully has all of mine down at the shop; Lenny's are right where they should be; but yours—most of yours haven't even chosen. How is this? They have no better purpose than to spend their energies tormenting each other? And you allow it?" He looked at Lenny, and then at Skyler. Then he turned back to Shelly. "If this is the way it's going," he said, "then you don't need me." He nodded at Lenny, took one last look at the rest of them, and left through the front door.

For a moment, nobody moved.

"Out with the old," Monkey finally said, looking around like he expected them to laugh. Nobody did. Nobody but Lance.

"Gotta go," somebody murmured. One by one, they left, stealing silent looks back and forth. Two minutes and the house was nearly empty.

"It still holds," Keele said, pointing at Baby before he left. "No matter what Edmund says." He nodded to Shelly, and then he left, too, Holt going out with him.

"Not as far as I'm concerned," Skyler said, poised in the hallway. He took a quick, scared glance, first toward Shelly, then at Lenny. The aps were waiting for Skyler in the hall. "I stand by you, Baby," he said, straightening himself up, "whatever happens." And then he was gone, too. Lenny hadn't moved from his place at the kitchen door.

Shelly shifted. He and Lenny looked at each other across the room, and Shelly smiled. Lenny's face didn't change. Shelly got up and stretched and walked across the room, down the hall to the door. "Later," he said, and he pulled the door closed quietly behind him.

Baby could feel Lenny's eyes on him.

Then Lenny pushed away from the wall and went into the kitchen. The water ran, and Lenny started messing around with the pans. It was not Lenny's night.

Baby stayed where he was, scared to go into the kitchen. He heard the refrigerator door open. Still, Baby stayed, his teeth clenched together. Lenny was loud with the pans, loud with the refrigerator, angry in his movements. Baby took a breath, went to the door, his hands shaking.

"It's my night," he said.

"Get out of here," Lenny snapped, and Baby got. He took his books and went to his room and sat on the bed, with the books leaning against his leg in a crazy pile. He picked one of them up, still hearing Lenny's anger, and opened it. But it was a long time before his mind caught up to what his eyes were reading.

ten

LENNY AND ROWENA BOTH WORKED
Saturday mornings; Baby had the house to himself. It
should have been good—a large chunk of peaceful, unin-
terrupted study time. But the quiet in the house made him
restless, and peace he didn't get; there was too much
going on in his head. Casey, for one thing—not just the
smell of her, or the flame that was her face; Baby couldn't
stop going over the things she'd said. About people being
afraid of him. About facing reality.

There was more to this than he could understand. And
the fact that his Presence seemed to do nothing these days
but hum with satisfaction only deepened his confusion;
the less comfortable he got, the louder the hum. The more
he thought about it, the more he wondered if everything
he'd ever believed was somehow slightly askew.

Two weeks ago, he'd just been unhappy. Now, things
were vastly more complicated. A week ago, he'd thought
Casey was a nice-enough girl, a surprise, a bit of a sociological revelation. Now, when he thought about her, every
nerve ending caught fire. He'd had unspeakable dreams
that left him staring at the ceiling through the darkest hours

of the night. And he still had the Clan to deal with.

Three days ago, Casey's parents—and everyone like them—had been, if not his enemies, certainly not his friends. But now, he'd talked to them; he felt responsible for them—and their kids and their neighbors. What's more, he kind of liked them. And kind of wanted them to like him. One thing he was certain of: He didn't want to do them any harm. Didn't want to confuse their lives, didn't want to answer their hospitality by messing around with their daughter behind their backs. The honorable thing would have been to withdraw.

But Baby couldn't do that. It was too late. And he couldn't see where things were going. He was headed downhill, no brakes, no steering, no visibility, picking up speed all the time.

He drank Maalox for lunch.

He decided to walk to Casey's. Another mistake. There was a lot more distance between them than he'd realized. And it was cold.

"You're an idiot," Casey said to him, pulling him in through her front door. "You want to end up in the hospital? Look at you. You're blue. Why couldn't you at least wear a stupid jacket or something? Why didn't you call me?" She took his books out of his arms and made him stand in front of the fireplace and then fussed over him until he got impatient with her. But all the time, he couldn't actually mind it.

Before he'd been there five minutes, the entire family had drifted in and settled themselves in the living room. Chase, absentmindedly pulling a clothespin off the sleeve of his sweater, hailed Baby like they were old friends and then sat down with the paper, jockeying with his wife for the business section. Peter had his head in the refrigerator, a wall away, and Sam was following Casey around like a sociable puppy.

Baby sat down at the table. Instead of sitting across from him the way she usually did, Casey slipped into the chair next to him—an almost frightening change—pulling the chair up close. And then Zack was on his lap, working his little fingers under the braided threads at Baby's wrist.

"Ow, Zack," Baby said, flinching.

"Zachary, get down," Casey directed.

But Baby put his arm around the little boy. "He's all right," he told her. He squeezed Zachary gently, glad for the solid warmth. "Just be careful, okay? You scratched me."

"Sorry," Zack said. He dropped his head against Baby's chest and stuck his fingers in his mouth, pulling happily against the braid.

"Why do you wear a bracelet, like a girl?" Sam asked, peering over Casey's shoulder.

"It's not a bracelet, Sam," Casey said quickly, taking a worried look at Baby.

He caught the look and sighed. "It's kind of a bracelet," Baby admitted. "My brother gave it to me, Sammy," he said.

"And why do you wear the same clothes every day?" Sam asked him. "My mom won't let *me* do that."

Baby laughed. "My mom won't let me do that, either," he said. "These aren't the same clothes. Just the same color."

"That's not a color," Sam decided. "It's black."

"Will you go play or something?" Casey asked him desperately.

"It's okay," Baby told her wearily. Casey's parents had stopped reading the newspapers they held; Baby could feel their focus like static electricity along the back of his neck. "Tell me something, Sam," he said suddenly.

"I'll tell you," Zack offered, mouth still full of fingers.

"You love your family a whole lot, don't you? More than anything."

"Yeah," Sam said as Zachary pulled the fingers out of his mouth to say, "A *course* we do."

Baby nodded. "Me too. I love my family a lot, even though . . ." But he couldn't finish that. "Thing is—could you guys be my friends, even though I wear black and you wear real colors? I'd really like that—if you were my friends. Even though we're different."

"Sure," Sam said, and Zachary affectionately stuck the wet fingers into Baby's eye.

"Good," Baby said softly, squeezing the little boy again and gently removing the fingers. "I do need friends." He kissed Zack lightly on the head. "You're lucky guys," Baby told them, putting the little boy down. "You have a beautiful life." He was a little surprised to feel Casey's cool hand slip softly into his. The newspapers rustled, but he found he needed to keep hold of her. Sam was dimpling up at him. He took a little breath. "You know, if we're really friends, you need to call me Baby. Nobody in my family calls me Thomas." He squeezed Casey's hand and let it go, nerves finally getting the best of him.

"Baby isn't a name," Sam said.

"Sam," Casey said, exasperated. "Will you leave him alone?"

"My mom called me Baby when I was little, so now everybody does." He looked at Casey apologetically. "Half the time, I don't know who you're talking to when you call me Thomas."

That nice color was coming up in her cheeks again.

She patted Sam without looking at Baby, and gave Sam a gentle push. "It's time for us to study," she said. "And we can't do it with you guys in here. You talk too much."

"Come on, guys," her father called. "We've got to clean up the den. Last one in there gets thrown in the cellar with the alligators."

Casey made a face. "Family tradition," she explained sweetly, pulling an imaginary little piece of something off Baby's sleeve. "We don't really have a cellar."

Casey's mom went into the kitchen and started running the water.

Casey looked at Baby, an odd little smile starting in her eyes, then turned away abruptly and started sifting through the materials on the table. "Where's my protractor?" she muttered. "Upstairs," she decided, dropping a book back onto the table. "You start," she directed him, now all business. "I'll be right back."

And she left Baby alone, staring at his math book.

Casey's mother was moving pans around in the kitchen like Lenny had the night before, making sharp, angry little noises with them, noises that made Baby flinch. Things kept happening that he just did not understand, and the constant undercurrents were beginning to wear him out. He took a steadying breath, stood up, and drifted over to the kitchen door, hesitating there, watching Casey's mother. Now she was putting dishes in the dishwasher. There was a clothespin stuck in a fold of her shirt, right in the middle of her back.

She glanced over her shoulder and saw him.

"I wonder," he said, swallowing, "if I could just get some water?"

"Sure," she said flatly. She opened a cabinet, fished out a fat green plastic cup, and filled it for him.

"You and Casey seem to be getting along pretty well," she said, handing it to him with no accompanying smile. So, it was exactly what he'd expected. Tutoring the Clan may have been awkward, but it was, at least, acceptable; getting personal with the Clan was another thing altogether.

He accepted the cup and looked down into it. He opened his mouth to explain, but then shut it again. She slapped her dish towel over her shoulder and started back in on the dishwasher.

"I'm not . . . ," he started, then floundered. He took a drink. She was looking at him. "We're getting along okay. I'm . . ." He took another drink. "You have a clothespin on your back."

She looked surprised, then annoyed, and reached for it. But it was smack in the middle and she couldn't get to it.

"I can get it," he offered. So she turned her back to him, hands on her hips. He pulled it off and she turned, her hand out. "Peter's a dead man," she swore, slipping the pin into her pocket.

"I don't want you to worry," Baby blurted. "If it's wrong for me to be here, I'll stop coming. I mean, I can understand." He tugged lightly at his shirt.

She pursed her lips. She half-turned back to the sink but then stopped and looked at him again, this time more gently. "Casey is one of my best friends," she said. "If you were a poor, sweet, wounded soldier in Flanders, and Casey was the good little English nurse, you'd be less dangerous." He blinked at her blankly. She laughed a little ruefully.

"If it makes you feel any better, Baby," she said, tripping over his name, "I never trust *any* of the guys who come around here after Casey. I tell all of you the same thing: Anything happens to her—you lay a *hand* on her—I'll find you, and I'll kill you. And I mean that. It *is* harder in this situation. Because of the complications. Because of the associations. Not because of you personally. Because, in spite of it all, I seem to find myself liking you."

He nodded, maybe a little happier now. He drank the rest of his water. "We're clear about Casey?" she asked.

"Absolutely," he said, and grinned shyly at her, then offered her the empty cup.

She gave him a reproachful look and pointed in the direction of the dishwasher. So he took the cup over and tried to fit it in.

"There," she said. She put a hand on his back and pointed. Then she gave his shoulder a little slap. "Now get out of here," she ordered, suddenly cheerful. "And get to work."

When Casey came back down, protractor in hand, Baby was righteously busy. "You're such a good boy," she said, patting his head. "And I think my mother likes you. But I do have to tell you—you've got a clothespin stuck on your back."

eleven

CASEY WAS MAKING HIM CRAZY.
He'd taken his mother to church on Sunday, tucking himself into the dark corner of an empty back pew during the Mass, and all he could think of the entire time was Casey, her eyes, her face, her hair, the touch of her, that clean, spicy smell. He wasn't aware of the building soaring up overhead; he couldn't hear his Presence anymore, could barely hear his own good sense. It was incredibly exhilarating, but it was also frightening, and he had no idea what he could do about it.

Lenny wasn't talking to him. Lenny hardly came into the house anymore. He spent all day Sunday in their garage working on some Italian engine, without ragging his mother about Baby. That alone was louder than anything Lenny could have said.

Casey behaved herself well enough at school on Monday, except for the way she kept looking at him—that light in her eyes, that innocent archness. Still, as long as she kept her distance and allowed him to keep his, there was balance.

But Monday afternoon at her house, she was horrible.

Every move she made, she was touching him—just a whisper of a brush across his arm, a slightly lingering pat on the back of his hand. And he couldn't look at her, because every time he did, her eyes were laughing and drawing him in. She set every nerve in his body on alert. But it was all done with such sweet naïveté, he couldn't believe she was aware of what she was doing. He was beginning to feel an unwilling sympathy for Gene Walenski.

She let Baby alone only when Peter walked through, or when her mother was close by, or when her father came in from work. Even through those moments, there was a binding of energy between the two of them, a tension that did nothing but get deeper as the afternoon went by.

She told him that she'd forgotten her physics book, so they had to work out of the same one. Which meant, in order to get any reading done, they had to lean over the book, both of them together—and when they did that, her hair fell down over her shoulder, curling softly against his arm. And he was breathing the green scent of her. About the thirtieth time she'd managed to cross her hand over his—ostensibly pointing out something on the far page, he slapped his hand down on hers and said, "Will you stop?"

She merely cocked her head and raised one eyebrow slightly, a sassy, unremorseful smirk. So much for direct protest. It was impossible. After two hours of it, he could hardly breathe. He finally pushed himself away from the table.

"Casey," he said. "I can't concentrate. This stuff is hard enough when I can. I'm going home."

She looked at him with mock gravity. "I'll stop," she said.

"Too late," he told her. His heart was thudding, and he

could feel the pulse of his blood in his palms and his ears, and in several other places. He got up and started putting his books together.

"Okay," Casey said, unruffled, "I'll take you home."

"No." Alone with her in that car. Terrifying thought.

"So, you're going to walk eighteen blocks in subzero weather with all those books and no coat?"

"I can call my brother." One lie. "Anyway, it's warm out there." Two lies.

She was looking at him reproachfully.

He sighed and put the books back down on the table. "Well," he said politely, "what do *you* suggest?"

She shook her head, mocking sympathy. But then she smiled—a clear smile with almost no coyness in it. "Come with me. Leave those," she said when he started to pick up the books.

"Casey," he protested doggedly as she went out into the living room. Her dad had just come in with the paper.

"Come," she said impatiently. She glanced at her dad. "We need a little break. If anybody asks, we're going out on the porch for a couple of minutes. Come *on,* Baby."

Baby got a sympathetic look from Chase. You don't know the half of it, Baby wanted to say.

"Jacket," Casey said, holding out one that must have been her father's. He thought it might be wise to refuse the offer, reasoning that the colder you were, the less time you spent outside. But she saw it coming and took no prisoners. "Put it on," she said. So he did.

With terrible misgiving in his heart, he followed her out through the front door, feeling the rush of warm air as it left the house with him. She hadn't even turned on the porch light. The only illumination out there was coming through the half-closed blinds in the windows.

Casey crossed the porch and sat down on the top step, settling her back against the railing. Baby didn't follow her that far. He stood shivering by the door, his hands deep in the pockets of her father's jacket.

"Will you just relax?" she said to him. "Will you come over here and sit down? I promise I have no ulterior motives, okay? I just want to talk."

He grimaced. And then he crossed the porch and perched on the railing opposite her.

"I'm not going to bite you," she said.

He laughed. He opened his mouth to say something, but couldn't quite work out what, so shut his mouth again. Then he gave up and sat down more or less beside her.

"Thank you," she said. "I feel much better now."

He did not take his hands out of the pockets of that jacket.

She was watching him. He was watching the shadows that were dancing across her front lawn. She sighed. He stared at his knees. She lifted a hand and very gently touched the tiny braid at his temple. "That's actually kind of barbaric," she said.

"Everything is barbaric," he said, flinching. "Depending on how you look at it."

And then there was silence.

"I'm sorry," she said finally. "Don't punish me for flirting with you, okay? I'm not doing that now. I just want you to talk to me."

He stole a look at her. She seemed contrite enough. "Casey—," he said, meaning to lecture her.

"I didn't know I was upsetting you," she said, cutting him off. "I certainly didn't want you to go Clan on me." She stole a look at him out of the corners of her eyes. "So, do you hate me now?"

He laughed and buried his face in one of his hands. Then he sat up again and drew in a slow, deep breath of the chilly air. "I don't hate you."

"Oh, thanks," she said. "So, why are you upset?"

"Upset," he echoed, and made the mistake of meeting those eyes of hers. "I'm not upset."

"Then why do you want to go home?"

"Casey," he said, looking down at his hands. "Let me tell you a story: When my mother was sixteen, she needed a ticket out—home was not good. So she got pregnant. And then she got married. And she got pregnant again four years later. Then she got divorced. And that was her life. After that, it was all work, all survival. She never got anything she wanted, except Lenny and me—and maybe that's pushing it. It was a ticket out of hell and back in through the other door."

He looked at her, hands still in his pockets. "I've seen what happens when people mess with serious things instead of just letting themselves be kids."

"Are you saying that's where you think I'm going?" she asked him. "Because that's way off. I'm just—"

"I'm not sexually active, Casey," he said abruptly. She shut her mouth, shocked into quiet. "The way I feel about it," he went on slowly, "it's all about commitment. Marriage—and family. But I'm not going to be married for a long, long time. Not till I can do it right. Not after what happened to my mom." He was studying his hands. "This is not a Clan attitude, believe me. And I pay for it all the time. It's a personal thing. But to me, it's absolute." He looked at her. "Does that make a difference for you?"

She was staring at him. "I'm not, either," she said, softly.

Some of the tenseness went out of him. "I didn't think

so," he said. "Something about you made me think not."

"Then why are you talking to me like this?" she asked. She was embarrassed; he couldn't see it, but he could hear it in her voice.

"Because of the things," he said, eyes closed, "you've been making me feel."

She didn't say anything.

"My life is hard enough," he said.

"I'm sorry," she told him.

"It's okay," he said, straightening his back. "Actually, I've been liking it." He laughed and ducked the slap she'd aimed at his knee. "But I can't afford it," he finished, shoving her hand back into her own territory. "So," he said, "what made you decide?"

"Decide?" she asked blankly. "Oh, you mean about . . . It's just part of what I believe. And my family. Right and wrong."

"General principle," he concluded.

"Yeah," she said softly. He nodded.

"There's so much to hope for," he said. "My mother never got a chance to figure out what her gifts were; she still wants to go to college—just to taste things, she says. Different things. She says, looking back, there's so much she should have wanted. So now, she wants it all for me," he said a little ruefully.

"Is that bad?" Casey asked him.

"It's hard," he admitted. "Everybody wants stuff for me; it's like, everything they do, they just do it to make sure I'm going to be happy. So, I kind of have to accept what they offer and be happy."

"Whether you are or not," Casey guessed. Baby shrugged, but that was to cover up the little wound he took when she put it like that.

"And what about you?" Casey asked him. "What do you want?"

He looked at her face, the smooth line of her cheek, the hollows in it—slight, rounded shadows that made her look soft and gentle. The exquisite detail of her eyes, dark lacing of lashes, hollows there, too, delicate lines. *Your eyes, your eyes.* She caught him at it, and she smiled and looked away from him. He wanted very much to touch.

"You're always asking me that," he said.

"Am I?" she asked. "Do you ever answer? Of course not."

He smiled down at his knees. "Otters," he started slowly, "are born knowing how to swim. But they're born on land. It's not until they're actually in the water that they know what they're meant to be. The moment they hit the water, everything about them makes sense. Can you imagine how that must feel, that moment of revelation?"

He pulled his hands out of his pockets and stuck them between his knees. "Lenny's like that with his engines," he said. "On a very deep level, they make sense to him, maybe make sense *of* him." He looked at her and was once again lost in the planes of her face. She couldn't stand the scrutiny and dropped her eyes. It was an artless movement that pulled up a tremendous sweetness inside of him.

"That's what I want," he said softly. "I figure, there's gotta be water for me someplace. Someplace I can make sense."

She nodded slowly, biting her bottom lip; then she looked at him. "Is that why you're doing this?" she asked.

"Probably," he said. He touched the soft, loose wisps that curled around her face, and then he passed the palm of his hand lightly across her cheek, across the airiness that was her hair. She closed her eyes.

The front porch light came on.

The front door opened. "Aren't you guys freezing?" Casey's father called. "Your mother says you *better* be freezing."

"We're freezing," Baby assured him.

"We were just coming in," Casey said. And then, "Baby's going to be good now and study, aren't you?"

"I probably should go home," Baby said, reaching for Casey's watch.

"Just another ten minutes," she coaxed, snatching her hand away, "and then I'll take you."

"I've got to go pick up some ice cream," her father offered. "I'll take him home. But you need to get in here before we freeze out the entire house." He disappeared, leaving the door open behind him.

"Will you go out with me?" Casey asked.

"No." Baby laughed. He stood up and offered her his hand.

"Why not?" She took his hand but did not get up.

"For one thing, because your family's insane. Anyway, what would be the point? We already see each other every day."

"But going out is different," she complained.

"Well, we can't afford anything different. And anyway, I don't have any money."

"I have money."

"Uh-huh," he said, trying to pull her up.

"Male pride," she said angrily, refusing to come.

"And everybody'd be saying, 'He's getting money off his rich little girlfriend.' I don't give anybody a chance to say I'm taking advantage of you."

"What if *I'm* taking advantage of *you*?"

"True as that may be, nobody's going to see it that way. Come on."

"Baby," she pled, "if we didn't have to worry about any of this stuff, would you?"

He laughed. "You mean if we didn't have to worry about pride and sex and politics and money? Sure. If we didn't have to worry about any of that, I'd go anywhere you wanted."

"You didn't take me seriously?" her father called from inside.

"We're *coming*, Dad," Casey yelled.

"They think we've been messing around out here," Baby said ruefully as Casey finally stood up. "Maybe we shouldn't have wasted it."

"Oh, well." Casey grinned at him, not giving him his hand back. "There's always next time."

"SO, YOU JUST had to go and do it." Joanna headed into the locker room, with Casey trailing along behind.

"Do what?" Casey asked absently.

"You couldn't just maintain a nice businesslike relationship, could you? You had to go gaga over him. You know what kind of a mess this is going to make?" Joanna dumped her books onto a bench and gave her lock a savage spin.

"Joanna, don't be stupid," Casey said.

"You think I'm blind?" Joanna turned to face her, hands on hips. She glanced around and lowered her voice. "You two sitting across the table at lunch, looking at each other like you're trying to suck each other's eyeballs out. Give me a break. And believe me, you're going to find out that *nobody* around here is blind."

Casey laughed and started working her own lock. "What would I do with his eyeballs?"

"Yeah, well," Joanna said, jamming her books into the locker. "He's been looking at you like that for days."

"He has?"

"Right, you didn't notice." The locker room was filling up. Joanna took a quick look back over her shoulder. "Take your time," she whispered to Casey. "We're going to be late today."

Casey started pulling off her shoes.

"I mean it, Case," Joanna said. "We need to talk right *now.*"

Casey scowled. Two, three minutes more they stalled around, waiting for everybody else to clear out. Lockers slammed and the room began to empty again.

"So, I'm saying you've got two serious problems here," Joanna said as the door closed for the last time. "And don't get that look with me, Case—I think you're the most kind, moral, intelligent, decent person who ever walked the earth, but I swear, sometimes you don't have a brain in your head. Problem one: Somebody's going to get hurt. Mr. Hall may have yelled at those guys for what they did on school property, but he sure can't do anything about what happens off school grounds. You don't hear the things I hear."

"Could we just not start this?" Casey warned her. "Do you want to know how many times I've gotten this from my parents?"

"So, it's not the way things ought to be." Joanna sailed right on. "I feel the same way you do about that. But it's

the way things *are*. Those guys are the way things are—
and no religion or legislation or theory of ethics is going to
change the fact that people still get hurt for really stupid
reasons. And I don't want it to be you. And I don't want it
to be your Baby, either, because I really like him." Joanna
plopped herself down on the bench beside Casey. "The
problem is, you're in love with him, huh?"

Casey looked down at her hands.

Joanna folded her arms. "And that's problem number
two. No question, this boy is, like, the ultimate romance—"

"Romance, right." Casey rolled her eyes.

"No, he's incredibly romantic—the suffering and silent
Dark Man with a Hidden Heart—'The highwayman comes
riding, riding—'"

"Joanna," Casey said sharply.

Joanna met her eyes squarely. "You can't deny there's
a mystic bond between you."

"We're colleagues," Casey said carefully.

Joanna chuckled. "Colleagues." Casey made an exasperated sound and started to move away. But Joanna
caught her arm. "Casey, if you don't face this honestly,
you're going to get into trouble. Because something could
happen. I can feel it."

"I'm seventeen years old, Joanna," Casey said scornfully. "It's not like I don't know right from wrong, and it's
not like I don't know anything about boys." But Joanna
just looked at her reproachfully.

"Okay," Casey said. "You want honesty? Fine. I . . . ,"
she began, but she couldn't finish it.

"You want him." Joanna said it so simply.

"That's not the point," Casey snapped.

"It's the truth. So just say it. Say it and deal with it."

"I'm not going to say it, Joanna. Anyway, what difference would it make what I want? This romance you think you're seeing—it doesn't exist. He won't go out with me. He won't even kiss me in the dark on my own front porch." She picked up a shoe and pitched it into her locker.

"I like him better all the time," Joanna declared. "At least he's got some sense."

Casey nearly spat. "The whole thing stinks."

"Of course it stinks. It stank for Romeo and Juliet, too. You think you're the only ones?" Joanna started to pry off her shoes.

"Well, too bad," Casey decided.

Joanna took a quick, worried look at her.

"If I want to go somewhere with him—a little, simple, innocent time with a friend," Casey said, jamming on her gym shoes, "I don't see why that should be anybody's business, including my parents'. Or is going to a movie some kind of sin now? Should I have to clear every little thing with my parents? I mean, by this time, shouldn't they trust my judgment? Don't look at me like that—didn't you just say you feel the same way I do?"

"Well, I don't think *exactly* the same . . . ," Joanna said.

"And if we have to worry about reality, then we'll just have to do something low-profile." She brightened. "Like we could go to the Pioneer—"

Joanna gasped. "You want to go to a drive-in? 'Simple, innocent time with a friend'?"

"It's just a movie," Casey said scornfully. "And nobody's going to see us there. Look, it's my last chance— the drive-in's closed after tomorrow night, and I'm never going to get him to take me anyplace that's public. I could go to your house tomorrow so we could finish the art project, and then I could sleep over. . . ."

But Joanna could see where this was going. "He won't do it," she said hopefully.

"He will if I put it to him right," Casey told her. And then she put her hand on Joanna's arm and fixed her with a look. "Are you my friend? Because if you really love me, you'll help me. You'll stand by me."

"Don't do that, Casey," Joanna said, sounding scared. "You're talking about going behind your mother's back. This isn't like you. Something's way wrong here."

"In or out?" Casey asked her.

Joanna pulled her hand away, exasperated. "In. Of course."

Casey nodded. "I needed you to say that."

Joanna scowled at her. "Yeah. Well, let's just hope you don't also need me to approve."

BUT THERE WAS NO right way to put it to Baby.

"No," he said, without waiting a heartbeat.

So she lied. "My parents won't mind," she said. And when he laughed at that, she pled, "We need this time. Besides, it would be good for—"

"The working relationship," he finished dryly.

"Yes," she said quietly. And then she looked at him soulfully. "Pleeeease?" And she was gratified to see him stopped in his tracks.

He said a little helplessly, "Your parents aren't going to listen past the word *drive-in*."

"My parents," she said with dignity, "trust me." And

then, "Look, how about this: If they say it's okay, we go; if they say no, then we don't."

He nodded slowly. "All right," he said. "If they say yes. Which I can't in any way imagine. But you've got to tell them this wasn't my idea, Casey. Please. I mean it."

"Absolutely," she said, and right about then, she should have been happy.

twelve

BABY WAS NOT COMFORTABLE WITH MIRACLES.
That Casey had actually sold the idea to her parents—
Baby would have sworn it couldn't happen. And that he
himself would end up with Lenny's car . . .

Too easy. But it hadn't really been that easy. He hadn't
exactly *lied* to Lenny—he'd just followed Lenny around
the garage, humbly handing him tools and talking about
the old days with the Clan, about funny things they'd
done, about how the Clan had always been his whole life.

In the end, he hadn't actually made any promises
about obeying the Clan word. But Baby thought he understood what was expected when Lenny finally handed him
the keys. And Baby had put out his hand for them, knowing the very act to be a lie, but not saying a word beyond
"Thanks."

Now Casey was sitting beside him, flicking him those
tight little smiles.

"Tell me *exactly* what your folks said," he asked for the
hundredth time, just making sure.

"They said it's fine," she told him over and over. "It's

fine as long as you keep your hands on the wheel." Which is exactly what he meant to do.

He pulled up under the box-office window and a kid leaned out, scanning the inside of the car. "Two?" he asked. He looked Baby over and then let his eyes slide past to Casey. "Hey, Casey," he said, taking the money Baby offered him.

"Hiya, Jason," she said without much enthusiasm. Jason was now checking out the paint job on the car.

"Sweet," he said. Baby smiled.

"You get your project done?" Jason asked Casey.

"Barely," she said. "Did you?"

"Had it done two weeks ago," Jason bragged. "Enjoy the movie."

Baby took the ticket stubs and smiled at Jason. "Thank you," he said, careful not to sound perfunctory. It won him a little closer scrutiny—the constant surprise that the Clan could actually speak. "Sure," Jason said, and waved them through. Baby sighed, feeling almost good now they were finally inside. Feeling, maybe, a little less jumpy.

"So, you haven't told me how you conned Lenny out of the car," she said, kidding.

Baby stiffened a little. "I guess he felt like this was a special occasion," he said carefully.

"Ah," she said, watching him. "Is it?"

"Isn't it?" he countered, and smiled at her. She smiled back, a little shy now. He started to pull into a place.

"Not here," she said quickly. "Go down past the refreshment stand." Her cheeks were a little flushed. "There. Right in the middle. See? It's perfect. Not too close—but right in the middle. That's my favorite place."

"Come here often?" he asked her, his voice prim.

"I used to come here with my family all the time," she said, just as primly. "And I have come here with other *girls*. And with whole *groups* of people."

He pulled up exactly between the speaker posts and shut down the engine. "Please, nobody spill a Coke on the hood," he said, closing his eyes. She started to roll down the window, going for the beat-up metal speaker box. "You can't hang that on the window," he warned, and he reached into the back for the clean chamois Lenny always kept back there. "Here, put this over the glass—just drape it over. And then we can hang the speaker on the inside. Kind of." He parted his hands helplessly. "It's Lenny's car," he apologized.

"Lenny's car," she murmured, beginning to sound a little more like herself. "Do we dare move around in here?"

"If you take off your shoes, and any and all metallic ornaments you might have hung or stuck about you," he told her grimly. "So, you've never been to the drive-in with a male person?"

She rolled her eyes provocatively and grinned, letting him suffer in her silence—which, he had to admit, was effective. She settled into the seat, and while she checked out the cars parked around, he was watching her. She had her hair in a couple of complex braids, tucked in close to her head but soft and fluted across her ears. Wisps stuck out all over, soft over her cheek and against her neck, making her look a little fuzzy. She caught him looking, the way she always did. He liked the way she colored up— that little grin she couldn't quite pull back.

"What do you see?" she asked, batting her eyelashes at him, mocking them both.

"A woman," he said crisply, doing the same.

"Oh," she said. "What kind?"

"A kind that asks too many questions," he told her. He picked up her wrist and twisted her arm around so that he could see her watch.

"Two minutes," she yelped. "I coulda *told* you."

"Sorry," he said, dropping her wrist. He folded his hands demurely in his lap. The screen up front began to flicker. "Your watch is slow."

"My watch is fine," she sniffed. The refreshment ads were now running.

"Don't even think about it," he told her, grimacing at cosmic images of dancing popcorn boxes and rapping Coke cans. "All my capital went into the price of admission. No feasting tonight, except spiritually."

She didn't mind. He hadn't expected her to. "This is a good movie, by the way," she said. "You'll like it."

His mouth hung open. "You've seen this movie?"

"Of course I've seen it," she said. "You think I'd go with a date to a movie I hadn't seen already? You know how embarrassing that could be?"

"I paid money for you to see something you've already seen?"

"I *liked* it," she said. "We *could* have gone somewhere else. We could have met downtown and sat at different tables and not said a word to each other. That way, nobody would have figured out we were together."

"Very funny," he said.

"But you know, maybe I've had this wrong from the beginning. It's probably *your* friends you're worried about. You just don't want them to see you with a girl like me. It'd ruin your reputation."

He grunted. "Too late. As you will recall, my friends

saw you last week. My reputation didn't suffer any."

"Oh, yeah?" she said, her eyes laughing. "So, what did they say about me?"

He thought about that. He changed gears and gave her a slow, male, Keele-like, waist-to-face perusal. She sat back against the door of the car, not so cocky for the moment. "Oh," she said.

He pulled the corners of his mouth up, not pleasantly.

"We're both in trouble, in other words," she said.

"You're very bright," he told her. The speaker crackled just next to her ear, and she jumped. "Movie time," he said.

It was a lousy speaker. The music coming out of it sounded like somebody crushing old shrink-wrap. "Wonderful," Casey murmured, settling down for the opening credits. Once the film started, she had to keep interpreting for Baby. Half an hour went by with Casey basically dubbing in all the parts. "Great movie," he remarked, yawning.

"It is when you can hear it," she said. "I'm freezing."

"I told you to bring your coat," he said.

"You never wear one," she pointed out.

"Maybe I don't have one," he said.

"Maybe you wouldn't wear one if you did," she said.

He smiled. "Maybe not," he agreed. "You want to go home?"

She shook her head and then continued to hug herself, shivering. He let out a hiss. "Fine," he said. He reached into the backseat; Lenny always kept a couple of nice fat, fluffy pillows back there. Baby got a strange feeling as he picked one of them up, thinking about why it was there and who might have used it during what. He stuffed it between the seats, stuffed it hard.

"You can sit on this," he said, but he was uncomfortable. "We really ought to go, if you're that cold. We could just go home and watch TV with your folks."

"Maybe in a minute," she said. "Maybe this'll work." She slid over onto the pillow and then shifted around, trying to get comfortable.

"This is stupid," he said. But then she settled herself, nestled against his side. His arm went around her shoulders. Involuntary. Innocent. Totally.

"Okay," he said, squinting at the screen, trying to ignore the smell of spice. "Let's see if we can get into this." But now his heart was beating a little quicker, and he was getting just a touch light-headed. "So, what's going on now?" he asked her, desperately trying to distract himself. "Who's that guy?"

"Han Solo," she said, burrowing in a little closer. She really was shivering.

"It's not Han Solo," he said. "Han Solo isn't born for another thousand years."

"What's his name? Indiana Jones. Jack Ryan. I don't remember his name."

"I *know* who the actor is, okay? I mean—okay, forget it. I'm totally lost." His heart was now beating just a little too fast, a little too hard. He looked down at her dismally. She was sitting so close, his heartbeat against her side must have felt like seismic activity. She peered up at him, grinning. "Yeah," he said, scowling at her. "You *like* this."

"Yes, I do," she said, and she reached up and kissed him on the mouth. He meant to tell her to knock it off. He meant to accuse her of leaving her coat home on purpose. He had every intention of telling her to get her seat belt on because he was going to take her home. But all he got around to doing was helping with that kiss. And another one. And then he felt those braids of hers under the palms of his hands and he wanted them out.

"Don't pull," she whispered, reaching back to help him. And then he let her do it, because his hands wanted the small of her back. He slipped his arms around her and pulled her in very gently, and he then kissed her on the neck, just below her ear. She made a tiny little sound and put her arms around his neck and then they were kissing again, and then again, until he felt like he was drinking her into himself, warm and sweet and incredibly intoxicating. A wave of heat hit him, and he suddenly felt urgency. He pulled her closer. Another deep kiss, and another flush of poignant heat, and then a heat that was deeper than anything he'd ever felt in his life.

Everything exploded in his mind at once, the things his hands ached to reach for—the rest of him ached to reach for, to touch, to fit against. They shouldn't have let her come. A tiny voice echoed somewhere at the back of his mind. This is exactly, precisely why . . . And then he remembered, very dimly, something she'd said about hands on the wheel. Both hands on the wheel.

He was nearly too hot to hang on to it. But hang on he did. He took both his hands off her and he found the wheel with them, taking great, dragging breaths of the cold air. He hauled himself upright in the driver's seat, holding on to that wheel as if it were the only fixed point in the universe.

"Get over there," he gasped, and then he sat with his eyes closed, pressing his head against the cold steering wheel, pulling in air like a drowning man. "Oh Lord," he whispered, his whole body shaking. He felt dizzy. "Don't ever do that again," he said between breaths. "Not ever again, Casey." She didn't answer him. He stayed where he was a long time—until things had cooled down, until the exquisiteness of the feeling had faded somewhat and his heart was beating only twice as hard as it was supposed to.

He took one last deep drink of air and, pushing himself up off the wheel, dropped his head back against the seat. A kind of warm little thrumming was going on somewhere at the back of his heart; by that, he knew he had done the right thing, and because of it, he was at peace with himself, if still a little light-headed. "Oh, man," he said, sighing. And then he turned to look at her.

She was sitting hunched into the corner of her seat, her face completely white, staring with incredible intensity at the dashboard.

"Hey," he said with some alarm. She didn't respond. "Casey," he said sharply, moving his hand her way. She jerked upright, and now she was staring at him.

"It's okay," he said. "Look, I'm sorry. You okay?"

She didn't answer him.

"Casey," he said, moving so that he could look straight into her eyes. "Nothing happened, okay?"

She looked at him, her face scared.

"What is it?" he asked her, the skin on his arms beginning to creep.

"I have to tell you something," she whispered. A terrible chill hit him about midstomach and spread.

"What is it?" he asked.

She was staring at him. "I lied to you about my parents."

It shouldn't have been a terrific surprise, considering where they were and how squirrelly she'd been acting. It was just that it had never even crossed his mind that she would lie. "They didn't say this was okay?"

"They didn't know. I lied to them, too."

"You never told them we were coming here?"

"I didn't tell them I was going to be with you."

He made a mirthless laugh. He felt like she'd hit him in the face.

"They think I'm still at Joanna's. That's why I had you pick me up there."

He pulled himself in, folding his hands together. "Okay," he said, in the face of its being absolutely and totally not okay. "Excuse me a minute," he said, and he opened the door of the car and got out. He leaned against the side of the car, still dizzy with what had gone on before, trying to see through an awful wash of humiliation.

A moment later, the door opened on her side, and they were looking at each other over the roof of the car.

He had his elbows against the car, his forehead in his hands, and that's the way he stood, looking at her, trying to come up with some way to tell her what she'd done. When she finally turned her back to him, he knew she was crying.

He put his forehead down on the cold metal of the car, reminding himself that she wasn't the only liar. He raised his head. She was still hunched up and looking as miserable as he felt. So he went slowly around the car.

"Casey," he said, clearing his throat. "You asked how I conned Lenny out of the car?"

She looked up at him and wiped a cheek with the back of her hand. "Yeah?"

"He thinks I'm finally . . ." But he couldn't finish it, and looked away. She blinked and then made a little moan.

He wanted more than anything to touch her then, but that warm little thrum of peace was still with him, saying he had better not. "We could just . . ." But what was he going to say? Just forget it? Just go home and act like nothing happened? Now we know we're both liars.

She had her arms folded in tight against her body. Her face was still wet, but she wasn't making a sound, and the silence was awful. She shook her head and looked away.

"It's almost funny," she said then, her voice thick. "Here's Baby, so confused. And Casey's so *sure*." She laughed—a thin sound. "But it turns out Baby's the only one who knows anything." She clenched her teeth. "Casey was supposed to be so *good*." She covered her mouth with a hand.

"Casey," he pled, "we didn't *do* anything."

"But I wanted you to," she said bitterly, glaring at him. "Don't you get it, Baby? I *wanted* you to."

See? her face was saying. He was getting little bumps up his arms and into his scalp. He took a small step back. "We didn't come anywhere close to that."

"Yes, we did," she said. "*I* did. I know what I felt."

"In the name of heaven, Casey," he cried, exasperated. "There's a huge difference between feeling something and doing it. You wouldn't do something you thought was wrong."

"Like I wouldn't lie to my parents?" she asked harshly.

"Will you knock it off?" he said. He reached out gingerly, meaning to pat her shoulder, but she jerked away from him.

"Don't," she said.

Somebody was running down the aisles between the cars. Casey turned just as Jason, the guy from the ticket booth, fell against the back of Lenny's car, both hands out to stop himself. Baby flinched, thinking of the paint.

"A bunch of guys just came in, looking for you," Jason said, panting. "They were drinking, and they sounded pretty ugly. I thought you'd want to know."

Casey gave Baby a quick, worried look, and suddenly, he couldn't remember what they'd been so upset about.

"Thanks," Baby said to Jason. He stepped back and opened the door, reached in over the seat for the ignition keys. He slammed the door and pressed the keys into Casey's hand. "You go with Jason to the ticket booth right now, and if we have to, you can come get the car later. Just take the car to your house, and Lenny'll come get it."

"What are you talking about?" she demanded, her eyes a little wild.

"Get out of here," he told her. "If for some reason I can't drive the car home, I want you to look after the car."

"I'm not going to leave you." She was outraged.

"Yes, you are," he said.

"Let's just go home," she said, throwing her hands out.

"Casey, you don't sneak out of a drive-in, okay? They'll just follow us out of here, and there are way worse places than this, Case; better here where we've got people around. I'll be okay. But not if you stay." She had that stubborn look, and it terrified him. "Tell her," he said to Jason.

"You better come with me," Jason said.

Then Baby saw the car—three rows over and down a little, cruising. "Casey," he said desperately, making her look at him. "I'm here because of you, okay? I was right about this. You owe me."

"Come on," Jason said, yanking at the back of her shirt.

"I hate this," she howled.

"I know," Baby said, nearly pushing her. "Go on. Go *on.*"

So, she allowed Jason to haul her along by the arm, looking back over her shoulder and stumbling as she followed. Baby watched until they'd disappeared around the corner of the refreshment stand, and then he hugged himself and leaned back against Lenny's red car, waiting, trying to settle his nerves.

The car slid along the next row. Baby watched, shivering, wishing Lenny and Edmund would somehow just suddenly materialize. Somebody in the car saw him. A dark face. Dickon. There was eye contact, but Dickon gave no outward sign. Then somebody else saw him and the car pulled into a place. Five guys got out.

Five cribs. All lettered. Four, if you didn't count Dickon. A couple of them were holding beer cans. One had a tire iron. "Lord," Baby whispered, too scared to move. *I don't want to do this. Don't make me go through this alone.*

Gene Walenski nodded, strolling along with his hands in the pockets of his jacket. "Look who's here," one of them said behind him, being cute. They were a car length away now, Dickon trailing along behind. The second Baby saw the worry on Dickon's face, he knew he was a dead man.

At that moment, the warm little thrum behind Baby's heart swelled into a sudden upsurging of warmth. Totally unexpected, white-hot and joyous, it staggered him so that he had to put a hand against the car to steady himself. No promise of deliverance, but it steeled him, and put the important parts of him, the delicate ones, somehow out of reach.

"Where is she?" Gene demanded. He came up alongside Lenny's car and leaned over, peering through the back windows. "Where is she?" he repeated, straightening up. He was close enough that Baby could smell the malt on his breath.

Baby looked at him evenly, keeping his mouth shut.

"Aren't *we* cool?" one of the others said. Gene jerked

his head, and his friends came up, making a little group around the car, a nice privacy screen around Baby and Walenski, Dickon on the outside of it.

"Gene," Dickon said. "She's not here. It was a mistake. Let's go."

"Three different guys saw her in the car with you," Gene said. "I want to know where she is."

"If you mean Casey," Baby said quietly, "she's not here."

Gene set his teeth and turned his face away, hands going to his hips. When he turned back, he spoke with very brittle patience. "Which is why I'm going to ask you only once more. Where is she?"

"Not here."

Gene's hands, hard fists, dropped away from his hips. He said a word under his breath.

"Man, Gene," Dickon said, trying scorn. "We got better business than this."

"She was with you when you drove in here, trash," Gene said, his eyes burning. "If she's not here now, I want to know why."

Baby said nothing.

"Maybe he just needs a little persuasion, Gordy," Gene said, nodding at one of the kids behind him, the biggest one—and Gordy moved quickly, much more quickly than Baby had expected. Baby grunted with pain as the kid twisted his arm and pinned it behind his back.

Your left arm, Baby started telling himself. Only the left one. It could be worse. He was shaking badly, and he was afraid they'd see it. He kept his face neutral and worked at keeping his breathing level.

"If you put one hand on her," Gene said softly, leaning into Baby's face, "I swear, I'll kill you."

Baby smiled at him. "You think you're so much better than I am?" he said. "You think she didn't tell me? You think everybody's like you?" Gene's face, flushed with the drinking, went nearly white, and he slugged Baby hard— a quick rock-fisted slam to the gut that would have doubled Baby over if big Gordy hadn't had his arm. Baby gagged, trying to drag air back into his body.

Baby was still coherent enough to see it when Dickon tried to jump on Gene's back. But the other two held him off.

"You and your little weird brotherhood," Gene hissed, down so close to Baby's face, Baby was sharing his breath. "You and your holy weirdness—you just stay in your place. We don't need you—you understand that—you and your suffering little attitude. You keep your hands off her. You stay in your swamp"—he hit Baby again, lower, harder—"and you keep your hands"—he hit him again— "and your filthy slime to yourself." He hit Baby one last time. Baby's knees gave out on him.

"Leave it," Dickon was yelling. "In the name of heaven, Gene . . ."

"Pull him up," Gene shouted as Baby buckled. Gordy hauled up hard on the arm.

When the bone gave, they all heard it. Baby heard it before he felt it. When he felt it, cutting through the terrible haze of his pain, it was the last thing he knew for a long time.

"YOU DAMN JERKS," Dickon shouted. He jumped forward and caught Baby before he hit the asphalt.

They were all standing there, staring.

Dickon glared at Gene and sank under Baby's weight until he was sitting on the ground, Baby limp in his arms.

"Why'd you have to break his arm?" Gene spat, scowling at Gordy.

"You told me . . . ," Gordy said. "How was *I* supposed to know the damn arm was gonna break?"

"Let's get out of here," Gene said.

And all the time, Dickon was saying, "I can't believe you did this. I can't believe I let this happen."

"We got to get out of here," one of them said, trying to hide his tire iron. "People are looking."

"He's gotta get to a hospital," Dickon snapped.

"I'm not taking him to any hospital," Gene said, going pale again. "It's not like this was *my* fault. Just dump him. Somebody'll call—"

"We take him, or I call the cops," Dickon said. Gene swore. "I mean it," Dickon said. "I'm not about to leave him here. Get the car." One of them grabbed the keys out of Gene's hand and ran.

"We'll take him to your house," Gene bargained. "If you keep your mouth shut about this. It's not like *I* was the problem here. I'm not getting stuff on my record because of *this*."

"What's my dad gonna be able to do for him at my house, Gene? Who knows what the hell you guys've done to him—it could be his shoulder. It could've been his *neck*. And you think my dad won't report this? You should have thought, Gene. Why didn't you listen to me?"

The car rolled up. Dickon bent over Baby. "You got guts and grace," he whispered, patting the good shoulder. "You deserve better than this. I'm sorry. I'm really sorry."

They loaded Baby into the backseat with Dickon, the

rest of them crammed in the front, and they started toward the exit.

"We either dump him in the mall lot or on your lawn," Gene said, looking at Dickon in the rearview mirror. "Because I'm not getting in trouble for this!"

As the police were already waiting for them by the exit gate, the question was fairly easily settled.

thirteen

BABY DIDN'T ACTUALLY COME TO HIMSELF
until somewhere between the hospital and home. He was
in Lenny's car; that much he knew. His mind was full of
pain and drug-obscured images, and he didn't understand,
for that first little while, what had been happening to him.
He remembered the police. He'd been scared of them,
thinking that somehow they were there because Casey's
parents had found out about the drive-in. He hadn't told
them anything, but he remembered that they'd kept asking
him something over and over.

And the hospital. And a doctor, and Dickon's face, and
Casey's. Their faces blending. Except she was crying. He
felt bad about that. And he was hurt and people kept asking him questions.

Nobody was asking him anything now. Now he was
huddled up in Lenny's passenger seat, holding his hurt arm
against his chest, his cheek pressed against the frame of
the door, just under the window. He had his eyes open,
and he was beginning to separate what he was seeing outside from what he was trying to remember. Lenny had the

radio on. His anger filled the car like a smell, but Baby closed his eyes and didn't care. The cast on his arm pressed into his ribs.

"I'm too tired, Len," he said, as if that explained everything.

When they finally pulled into the driveway, Baby was more awake than not. He got out when Lenny opened the door, but his knees buckled under him, and he needed help getting to the front door of the house.

"Just stay here," Lenny ordered, his voice low. And he went on down the dark little hall into the front room, leaving Baby to shiver at the door. Baby could hear a murmur of voices, and then his mother's voice, loud. "Come on," Lenny said, materializing beside him. "Let's get it over with."

Baby's mother was standing in the middle of the living room, her face pale. "What happened?" she asked them.

"He had an accident," Lenny said.

"A guy broke my arm," Baby said, suddenly remembering and too tired to do any more equivocating.

"Why?" his mother asked hollowly. "Was this a gang fight?"

"No," Baby said, his voice slurry. "It was a personal matter."

"Who?" she asked.

"Forget it," Lenny said. "He wouldn't tell the police. He won't tell me. He's sure as hell not going to tell you."

"Why not?" his mother asked. "Why wouldn't you tell them?"

"Why be Clan," Lenny asked him, anger clear in his voice, "if you don't let it take care of you?"

"You should have told the police," his mother said.

"If I tell you," Baby said to Lenny, remembering there was a reason, "the next thing, somebody gets hurt. Somebody's going to end up hurt."

"Yeah," Lenny said. "And it was you."

"Then that's enough," Baby told him.

"Let us help you," Lenny pressed. "We'll kill those guys for this."

"No," their mother said, sounding scared. "Baby's right. Let the police take care of it."

"I'm not going to," Baby said to Lenny. "I can't do that."

Lenny threw up his hands and stared at the wall, ridges in the muscles along his jaw.

"Something else," Baby said, still piecing things together. "I lied to you this afternoon, Len. To get the car."

"Lied about what?" his mother asked.

Lenny's eyes, dark and unreadable, locked with Baby's.

"I'm not going to do that, either," Baby told him, trying to make the words clear. "You should just tell them. The girl's my friend. Anyway, I'm not messing with anybody's life just to keep the Clan. Not even for you. It'd be wrong. And I'm not going to do it."

His mother had gone silent.

"Fine," Lenny said.

Baby pressed one hand flat against his stomach. The medicine they'd given him must have been wearing off; his arm hurt and there was a deep ache in his gut. He had to blink to keep Lenny in focus.

"When you take those clothes off tonight," Lenny said coolly, "you fold them up and put them on the dresser."

"What?" Baby asked, not quite getting it.

"And you take the rest of those clothes I bought for

you, and do the same. You make a pile. I'll take them and give them to somebody else in the morning."

"You're going to give somebody my clothes?"

"You're on your own," Lenny said.

Like Lenny had just hit him.

"Just because I let somebody break my arm?" he asked, definitely losing grip on his balance.

"You heard me," Lenny told him.

"No, Len—" Baby put his good hand out, desperate, trying to sound so reasonable.

But Lenny was picking up the scissors that'd been lying on the couch beside their mother's mending.

"Lenny, don't," Baby said sharply, taking a step back. But Lenny kept coming, his face dark and set, and Baby went to his knees.

"Not on your knees," his mother cried out.

Baby was begging now, "Please, Lenny. Please, Lenny." And he was still begging when Lenny cut the braid out of his hair. "Lenny," he cried then, but his brother threw the scissors onto the couch and walked out of the room without another word. They heard it when the tiny braid hit the bottom of the metal trash can. The back door slammed. Baby stared after his brother, stunned, his arm aching like fire. And then he put his face on the floor.

THERE WAS NO SOUND in the room, only Baby, trying to breathe through a terrific pressure in his chest. When he pushed himself slowly, heavily, back up onto his knees, he was vaguely puzzled.

His mother was sitting on the couch, mending one of Lenny's shirts. He squatted on his heels, dully, watching her. Something had happened. He thought it had. But he most carefully and absolutely couldn't remember it now. She looked down at him over her work, and he was shocked at the intensity in her face. He pressed one hand flat against his chest.

She studied him thoughtfully for a moment. Then her face went pale and she glanced toward the dark kitchen. She dropped her work on the couch and took off her glasses. "I need to go to church," she said briskly. At first, he didn't understand her. She stood up and started for the front closet.

"Oh, Mama," he said. "Maybe another time. Maybe tomorrow, okay?" The floor kept moving under him. "I'm just so tired."

She stopped and regarded him—took one more look at the kitchen, as if she was afraid of what might be in there. Then she seemed to master her face, and she smiled tightly at him. "It's all right," she said with transparent lightness, reaching for her coat. "You go on to bed." She glanced at her watch. "It's not even ten-thirty. I won't be more than an hour. I'll check you when I come in." As though she believed he'd let her go alone in the dark. As though he ever had.

"Okay," he said, brokenly, holding his hurt arm and trying to get up off his knees. "Just let me get my coat—I don't think I can get on my coat." She held his jacket out to him, her face set. He got to his feet. "Just a minute," he said, and he went down the hall to the bathroom. He leaned against the bathroom wall for a moment, and then he flipped the toilet seat up and had dry heaves.

He sat on the edge of the tub afterward, knees gone limp, and then he made himself get up. He stopped to lean against the wall once more, running a hand over his eyes.

He was freezing. He pushed off the wall and went back to the living room, where his mother was waiting.

"I'm not sure I can make it all the way there," he said hoarsely.

"I know," she said. She looked close to tears. "I told you—you should go to bed. Baby, I'm not asking you to do this."

He groaned inside himself and made his way over to the front door. "Come on," he said. She draped his jacket gently over his shoulders. She took his arm and steered him out onto the sidewalk. Once they were out there, she slipped her arm around his waist, as though she thought she could support him that way. The cold air braced him up a little, but he did the distance in what was half a dream, putting his last reserves into keeping his legs under him.

"They wanted you to make love to your girl," she guessed after a while.

He squinted into the dark, trying to remember. "Did they?" he asked stupidly. Then he recalled, "It was a test."

"You failed it," she concluded.

"I think so," he said. Her arm tightened around him. He felt a little like he was floating, and the play of lights against the night shadows confused him. She was speaking, but for a while he couldn't quite catch it.

"We'll get you some clothes," he heard her say.

But he didn't want to talk about that. He pulled himself in very tight, and he started counting his steps, concentrating on what his feet were doing.

"I'll call my cousin Katherine when we get home," his mother went on. "You can borrow some stuff from Dwight."

Baby had a sudden and almost irresistible urge to

throw a fit, right there on the street. "Not *Dwight*. Dwight looks like an idiot."

His mother laughed. "That never seemed to bother *you*."

He stopped.

"Why are we here?" he asked her, shaking with the cold. "Why am I out here? I'm sick. I should be lying down. I need somebody to take care of me."

She turned to him, but her face was all shadow. "I am taking care of you," she said softly. "The best I know how. You needed to get out of that house. We needed to clear your head. Come on, honey." He let her pull him along. Whatever it was she thought she was doing, it was beyond him to understand it.

When they came to the cathedral steps at last, she let go of his arm and went on up, leaving him behind on the sidewalk. He looked up that stone stairway and took the stairs one at a time, doggedly. When he finally reached the top, he had to rest, too dizzy to move away from the railing.

She was waiting there for him, and she heaved at the great door, holding it open. She stood with the light behind her, like a halo, smiling as if she thought she were an angel offering him refuge. He passed over that threshold, grateful that he hadn't had to pull the door open himself. The vestibule air was warm and gentle on his face. The dark beyond was welcoming. She stood behind him, watching as he made his way slowly into his old place in the back, settling himself gingerly against the great stone wall. He closed his eyes and let himself down until he was sitting on the floor. It was chilly and there was a draft, but he was past caring.

Something is wrong, he told the Presence. Please don't

let me hate them. Because I'm afraid I do. All of them. Please. Please. My arm hurts very much.

It was quiet. Baby closed his eyes. Mother, don't stay too long. But there was no telling with her, no telling how long it would take.

THE NEXT THING HE SAW was the wall of his own room. He had no idea how he'd come there. It was morning, because it was light. And he was late for his session with Mr. Belnap.

fourteen

CASEY SPENT THE REST OF THE
night at Joanna's. Not to say that she slept.

The next morning in homeroom, somebody new was sitting in Baby's seat. The terrible night, and then this—as if he'd died and they'd already filled in his place. As if he'd never really been there at all. She stood stupidly in the doorway and stared.

Then she saw the cast on the boy's arm and took a harder look, coming slowly into the room. And it turned out to be Baby, sitting there in some kind of blue pants and a mushy striped polo shirt.

He didn't look up when she sat down. He wasn't looking at anything. He was sitting there in that weird getup, blank-eyed and isolated, just like at the beginning. Freezing Casey out. And why not? Liar. Hypocrite. Betrayer. She wanted to put her head down on the desk and howl.

Joanna came in the room a second later. Her eyes widened when she saw Baby. Casey made a quick quelling gesture and Joanna, subsiding, went to her own desk.

The bell rang and the room began to quiet. Casey didn't look around to see who else had shown up. She was afraid of seeing Gene; she was afraid she'd stand up and throw things and scream at him right there, in front of everybody.

The lecture started. She opened her notebook. Baby did not open his. Baby didn't move at all for the first fifteen minutes of the class. His face was rigid and unnaturally pale. Casey kept sneaking short worried glances at him all through the lecture, as did Mrs. Thurman. By the end of the class, Baby had his head down on the desk, his arm cradled in his lap. When the bell rang, he didn't stir. Casey waited as long as she could stand it; then she reached across the aisle and touched him timidly, saying his name.

He came up all at once, staring at the space in front of him, as though she'd jerked him out of a terrible dream. That's when she noticed the little braid with the beads was gone. Somebody had obviously cut it out of his hair. She was hoping fervently he had done it to himself. So there'd been more to last night, after the hospital. Another awful, terrible thing.

He stood up, ineffectually fumbling at his books with one hand. It was all she could do not to help, and her eyes filled with tears, watching. He finally headed down the aisle; he hadn't even glanced her way. Casey looked at his desk and chilled. Two of his books were still sitting there.

She grabbed them and jumped up to follow him, but there were too many people between them, and she couldn't reach him. She kept her eyes on him, trying to work her way through the kids.

Gene's friends got to him first. They pushed Baby back against the open door just as he was going out, putting pressure on the hurt arm. The kids in front of her came to a slow, stupid stop, watching.

"Hey," Casey heard one of the boys saying. "Nice shirt." He lifted Baby's cast as if to get a better look at the clothes. Baby went totally white.

"Get your hands off him," Casey shouted.

Mrs. Thurman's head came up. "Boys," she barked, coming out of her chair.

Gene was standing out in the hall, watching. "If you think the nice shirt's going to make any difference," he said conversationally, "dream on. Everybody knows what you are." His friends had followed him out into the hall, laughing and bumping up against Baby every chance they got. Then they were gone, and Baby was backed against the door, white-faced and blank, as though somebody had pinned him there. Casey got to him just before Mrs. Thurman did, but then stalled out, realizing she didn't have any idea what to do for him.

"We're hurting, aren't we?" Dickon said from just behind her. "Didn't you take your medication this morning?" A little intelligence flickered in Baby's eyes, but he made no answer.

"Idiot," Dickon said. "Come on. We'll take care of him, Mrs. Thurman. Let's get you out of here. Catch his books." With a nod at the teacher, he took Baby's good arm and directed him out into the hall, leaving Casey to follow.

"So why are you here, anyway?" Dickon asked, guiding Baby along.

"Math test," Baby murmured. "I can't afford to miss." There was a muzzy fragility to his words, as though he had a headache and didn't want to jolt himself.

"Being here doesn't guarantee you're not going to miss anything," Dickon pointed out grimly. "My dad would kill you if he saw you walking around like this today."

Casey trailed along unhappily. "Baby," she said, but he didn't seem to hear. "Baby," she repeated, catching up. The words came out in a desperate, unhappy rush. "It's my fault. The whole thing. You were right. Everybody was right." And now she was crying, right in the middle of the hall.

Then he stopped. Just stopped walking. People practically piled up behind him, it was so sudden. He stood still, his breathing shallow and his color terrible. Dickon put a hand in the middle of Baby's back, looking into his face. Baby moistened his lips carefully and closed his eyes. "Maybe you're right," he whispered, then swallowed. Kids streamed around them until the halls started to empty out. A few last kids cruised slowly by, hoping to see something interesting.

Dickon picked up Baby's hand. "You're freezing," he said. Then, to Casey, "Help me." They walked Baby over carefully so that he could lean against the lockers. Baby was chilling hard now. Casey stared at him over Dickon's bracing arm.

"You can't still be in shock," Dickon said, looking worried. "Something else has got to be going on here. Listen," he told Casey, "get some passes and find his address, and I'll get this martyr out to the car, okay? I'm in B lot, over toward the field. We'll wait out there for you. But you got to hurry, okay?"

Casey accepted the order silently.

DICKON PUT HIS SHOULDER under Baby's good arm and started for the outside door. It was slow going. Whatever had been holding the kid together was definitely coming unraveled.

"Sorry," Baby panted, resting by the door before they went outside.

"I don't need your apologies," Dickon said sharply. He stripped off his jacket and put it over Baby's shoulders. "You going to faint?"

"No," Baby said, probably lying. They started out toward the lot. We can make it, Dickon thought, seeing the set of Baby's face and remembering it from the night before. He took a little more of the weight onto his own shoulder.

"Sorry," Baby whispered again.

"Look, shut up, all right?" Dickon said to him. "Don't apologize to me."

He puffed along, weaving through the lines of parked cars until he could finally unload Baby against the body of his dark blue Honda. Dickon fished in his pockets for the keys. "Okay?" he asked. Baby nodded, still chilling, silently cradling his bad arm.

Dickon found the keys, unlocked the back door, opened it, pocketed the keys, and then faced Baby. "Look," he said. "I wish . . . I should have done something last night."

Baby opened his eyes and looked back at him. "Okay," he said hoarsely. "You should've done." And then he laughed—a short, painful sound. "Done what?"

Dickon looked away.

Baby smiled sloppily. "I'm not dead. I owe you that."

Dickon flinched. "Don't," he said angrily. "Come on." He took Baby's good arm and worked him into the back-seat. "Lie down," he ordered. "I'm going to put this under your feet." He balled up his jacket and waited. Baby stretched himself painfully along the seat. Dickon tucked his jacket under Baby's feet and then fastened a seat belt loosely around his body. He stood back and slammed the back door; then he had to find his keys again and let himself into the front. He slid in behind the wheel, jaw tight and eyes stinging.

"Look," he said, jamming the keys into the ignition. "Just don't say you owe me."

"Fine," sighed Baby. "I forgive you."

Dickon put his palms against the wheel and pushed. He held the pressure and then released it and put his head back against the seat. When he glanced back, Baby was lying quietly in a pool of sunlight.

Just then, Casey came around the corner of the building, looking for the car. He rolled down the window and waved to her; she waved pink slips back at him. He started the car as she climbed in. "Mr. Hall kept asking questions," she told him, pulling her belt across. "He heard about last night, but he thought it was some gang thing."

"He was right," Dickon said grimly, and pulled away. Casey stuffed herself into the far corner of the seat and stared out the window.

Dickon glanced at her. "You're real happy," he said.

She ignored him.

"He's not going to die," Dickon said. "It's just the trauma. I hope. I hope he's not, like, bleeding inside."

Her eyes went wide.

"He's not," he said quickly. "My dad would have caught it last night. Don't worry about it." He pulled to the head of the driveway and hesitated.

"Left," she told him. "And then left at the light." A moment later, she asked, "Did you ever lie to your folks, Dickon?"

"Not lately," Dickon said, pulling out.

"Don't ever do it," she said sadly. "It's awful." She bumped her head softly against the glass. "That whole thing was my fault."

"What do you mean?" Dickon asked. "You mean last night? Just how do you figure that's your fault?"

"Right at the stop sign and then all the way down to the Safeway. After that, I don't know. I've never been to his house." She studied the paper she held in her hand, and then she looked up, grimacing. "It was my fault he was there. He told me it was stupid, but I had to have my own way. I always have to have my own way. The thing I don't understand is—I don't understand why Gene had to do this."

Dickon sighed.

"You were with him," she said. "You've got to explain this to me."

"You think I can explain it?" Dickon asked her. "How can I explain it? I never jumped anybody in my life. But I gotta tell you—there *is* something about those Clan guys that makes you want to push their faces in. The attitude—like they're just one big in-your-face. The guys were talking about it last night, driving around, drinking beer and talking about how they'd just like to walk into that Clan Special Ed room and put some heads together. Then somebody told Gene about seeing you in that car with him. Gene went nuts. I think he still . . ." He shrugged. "But what's the difference why? This should never have happened. Not here. Not with people like us. There's just no excuse for it."

She leaned her forehead against her window and said soulfully, "I hate letter jackets."

Dickon took a quick look at her. "No," he said. "Casey, I worked real hard for the jacket. It's not the jacket. It has nothing to do with that." She looked at him silently.

He drew up by the Safeway and waited. "Two more blocks," she said, checking her notes, "that way."

He drove on, peering up at the street signs. "Which one?" he asked.

"Here," she said. "Left, I think." She checked the paper once more, and then squinted at the house numbers as he cruised. "That one," she said, pointing out a tiny pink house with a nonexistent yard and a big garage. Dickon pulled in against the curb and shut off the engine.

THE LIGHT WAS WARM against Baby's eyelids. Nice.

Lying in the backseat of a car was a very simple thing; they'd put him here, and now they were taking him somewhere. The talking up front—low, sonorous music—kept putting him to sleep around the pain. None of it was his responsibility.

It was a deliberate thing, remembering, not remembering—holding things just out of reach. The pain helped. He couldn't remember where he'd been, except that he'd been someplace. There'd been some talking, but that was over. As long as he never actually got anywhere, things would be just fine.

Now the car turned, the sun left his face, and he was cold all over. Cold inside. He'd had an awful kind of pressure in his chest for a long time. He was worried about that. It made breathing hard. It was mostly what he'd been doing all day, breathing through that pressure. And dancing around the hot spots in his head.

The car stopped.

"We got you home," a girl said. The sun was on his feet now. The door by his head came open.

"Come on." Said to him? To her? Pulling on him—to him, then. He pushed himself up, being so careful about the arm.

"Can you get out?" they were asking him. And he could, but he had to do it carefully. "Come on," the girl said gently. The kindness in her voice made things harder. He let them pull him up. He heard the car door close behind him, and then they were all walking, the two others sort of shoving him along between. The sun was on his back.

There was a tremendous noise—machinery, whining and screaming. They all looked toward the garage. Sparks were flying behind the windows. The moment he saw that, Baby went icy with fear.

"Good," Casey said. "His brother must be home. I know his mother works."

His brother's home. The breathing suddenly got very much harder.

"You okay?" Dickon asked him, pulling on him, pulling him toward the house. "I don't like this," Dickon said. They went up the steps and one of them opened the door.

It was colder in the house. And something already very strained was starting to swell.

"What do you think we should do?" she asked. "Just put him to bed, I guess."

But they didn't. They put him on the couch, and then

they came and went. Somebody was on the phone. Somebody covered him with something.

Baby lay where they put him, all his senses fixed on the garage. He was freezing, except his arm and his gut were one deep, searing ache. He opened his eyes and everybody was gone. Casey came through the hall door with another blanket. Casey, who had lied to him. "You still cold?" she asked him. He just looked at her. She tucked the blanket in all around, and then she settled back on her heels, looking at him. The sun came in through the side windows and lit up her hair.

"Are you going to be okay?" she asked him. But he didn't open his mouth. "You're scaring me," she said.

"Where're the pills?" Dickon asked, standing behind her.

"I'll go look," Casey said, pushing herself up away from the floor.

"You eat anything today?" Dickon was asking. "Probably not, huh? Of course not. For somebody who's supposed to be a whiz kid, you don't have much upstairs, do you?"

"I found them," Casey announced.

"See if you can find him a piece of white bread or some crackers or something. No wonder he looks like a zombie." Dickon scowled down at him. He said more, but Baby closed his eyes so he wouldn't have to hear it. Then they were trying to make him eat crackers. But he wouldn't. His stomach lurched at the sight of them.

"Maybe we should go get his brother," Dickon said.

Baby's eyes came open. "No," he whispered. His breath was so quick now, he wondered if he was going to be sick. He surrendered, putting his hand out for the crackers. He could have cried. They gave him three.

"Let's just write him a note," Casey said. "I don't want to talk to his brother again." She wasn't looking at Dickon.

"Then I will," Dickon said, and started looking around for the way out. "We need to talk to him."

"No," Baby said.

"Why not?" Dickon wanted to know.

"He's working," Baby croaked. "I'm okay." They both looked down at him doubtfully.

"You're not," Dickon said.

"It's okay," Baby pled, muzzily.

"You scared of your brother?" Dickon asked.

Baby didn't answer for a beat. "No," he said. "You can go."

"I don't like it," Dickon said.

"I want to sleep," Baby lied.

"I think it'll be okay," she said. "His brother was really gentle with him last night at the hospital. I'm going to write him a note."

"What if he leaves?" Dickon called after her. "He doesn't even know Fairbairn's in here."

"Baby," Casey corrected him from the kitchen. "That's what they call him."

"I thought that's what you called him," Dickon said.

"He'll come in," Baby pled. Things were beginning to come back to him rapidly now, and with awful clarity. "You should go."

"Well, let's give him the pills, anyway," Dickon said. Which meant they had to sit him up and give him the water, and wait until he'd swallowed. "I'm serious," Dickon told him as they eased him down again. "Stay there. Okay?"

"Okay," Baby said, swallowing, hugging himself so

they wouldn't know how hard he was still shivering.

"I don't like to leave him like this," Dickon said. Baby closed his eyes.

"Neither do I," Casey said quietly. "But that's what he wants, isn't it, Baby?" A second later, she said, "Come on, Dickon."

Baby kept his eyes screwed shut until the front door closed softly behind them. Then he opened his eyes and stared at the ceiling, letting go of a sob.

"Lenny," he whispered, because he was remembering everything now. He lay in the quiet house, shivering and remembering it all, and there was only the sound of the clock in his mother's bedroom, and the muffled pulsing of his brother's compressor.

"Lord," he pled, but Baby's heart was past hearing, the pressure around it so horrible now, Baby had to sit up to breathe. "All right," he whispered. "All right." And he pulled himself up onto his feet. He leaned against the arm of the couch, blinking, and then he straightened up and went to the back door, taking it one step at a time.

One step at a time out to the garage, a thousand steps, with blood beating in his ears. He finally propped his good arm against the rough wall of the garage and put his head against it. He could feel the beat of the compressor through the wall.

He composed himself, and then he pushed open the side door and, leaning against the jamb, let his eyes adjust to the dimness inside. Lenny was there at his bench, parts and machines and tools piled all around him. A shower of sparks flew up from the bench. Lenny had his back to the door, and Baby could barely tell where the man and the darkness separated.

"Lenny," he said. The machines should have drowned

him out. But Lenny froze the moment Baby spoke. And then he turned his head slowly, lifting his visor.

Baby pressed one hand over his heart, holding himself together, and cleared his face of everything, the way Lenny had taught him to do. And then he spoke. "All my life," Baby said, "I wanted to do right for you." He still couldn't see very clearly. "I loved you, Len. I tried. I learned everything you wanted me to. I never got in your way. I wanted to be what you wanted. I tried, Lenny. But I"—he blinked—"I couldn't cut it. I let you down. I'm sorry."

Lenny hadn't moved.

Baby swallowed and pushed away from the door frame, half-turned toward the house. Then he stopped, and he spoke again, without looking at Lenny.

"Those guys. This morning, they laughed at these clothes. They thought I left the Clan so they wouldn't hurt me anymore. I thought you'd want to know—if it was humiliation you were after, you got it." He turned his back to the garage, walking carefully, slowly, across the driveway. Now that he had let the thing be real, he was starting to come apart, seams in very important places finally tearing loose.

Back stairs, back door. He got through the kitchen, but there he had to stop, leaning heavily against the door frame, helplessly suspended between the kitchen and the living room.

The compressor went silent.

Baby was afraid to breathe.

The back door opened behind him, and Lenny came quietly into the house. For a long moment, there was silence. And then Lenny spoke.

"You don't understand, Babe," he said.

Baby Brother hung on to the wall and didn't move.

"When you were a baby—I still remember this—you were lying in that little bed in Mom's room. And I came in to look at you. The baby. Big deal. You looked at me—you know, that goofy way babies look at stuff. And for some reason, I put my finger out to touch your hand. The second I touched you, you grabbed my finger with your little hand."

Baby swallowed. Now his face was coming apart, and there was nothing he could do.

"I felt something—like it hurt me. And I thought, This is *my* baby. Because all of a sudden, I thought you loved me. And, as far as I knew, nobody else ever had."

Baby pressed his forehead into the wall.

"So that's how it was going to be with us. I was going to take care of you. We were going to do it together. I'd be there first, and I'd wait, and I'd make sure you knew everything you needed to know, and I'd make sure you were okay.

"That's what the Clan was for. Shelly had his own ideas, and so did Edmund. But that was it for me. And it was good for a long time. But then Edmund started warning me, 'He's different than you. He needs different things than you, and sooner or later, you're going to have to face it, or you're going to hurt him.' But I didn't want to hear that. I thought maybe you were going through phases, you know. Like, you'd get through it and you'd settle down. And then we'd go into business, and I could—"

Lenny stopped.

"But he was right," he went on softly. "I don't understand you half the time. Hell, you think sex is some kind of religious ritual." Lenny laughed. But there was no humor in the sound. "Your mother's right. I can't help you anymore. I don't even know where you're going. I know the Clan is wrong for you. You try to fit; you kill yourself trying to fit—because it matters so much to *me*. It makes me sick to watch it.

"I don't know why the hell I gave you the car. If you'd come in here and told me you'd actually done that girl—*you*—I would have killed you, Baby Brother. And if I hadn't been so damn stupid, this thing wouldn't have happened."

Lenny moved a chair. When he spoke again, his voice was low and sad. "The whole thing's coming apart. I should have seen it a long time ago. But I'm too stubborn. Too stupid. I didn't want to see my life falling apart." Baby could hear the chair give as Lenny leaned on it. "I love you, Baby Brother," he went on gently. "I always have. But I'm not good for you, Babe. I guess I finally had to face it last night, seeing you at the hospital like that. Putting you on your own was not supposed to be a punishment, Babe. It hurt me like hell." He faltered and went silent. When he went on, his voice was rough. "I had to make myself set you free. You understand?"

Baby sobbed. "I don't want it," he said. "You're my brother."

Lenny came up behind him and, taking him by the shoulders, turned him around. "I'll always be that," he said, and he put his arms around Baby and held him, held him for a long time because Baby was finally disintegrating. Then Lenny saw the note Casey had written, picked it up off the kitchen table, and read it through. "Great," he said. "Time for bed."

Lenny took Baby to his room. He put Baby on the bed and undressed him, handling him gently. He covered Baby up and then went hunting for blankets. While he was gone, Baby had the terrors. Lenny came back in and tucked the blankets around him, saying quiet things. Then he stood beside the bed, looking down.

"Don't leave me, Len, okay?" Baby begged.

"All right," Lenny said. He got himself a chair and put it close to the bed. Then he sat down and picked up Baby's hand, and stayed there while Baby finally worked through the worst of his grief.

fifteen

" B A B Y ?

"Baby, honey?"

There had been a dream.

Somebody touched him on the shoulder, and he yawned.

"Honey, I'm sorry to wake you. . . ."

Baby groaned and palmed his eyes. The room was dark. Light streamed in from the hall, and somebody was silhouetted in it. "Lenny?" he asked. "What time is it?"

"About eight-thirty," his mother said. She sat down on the edge of the bed. "How do you feel?" She brushed at his hair with her fingertips.

"I don't know," he moaned. "Is it still today? Where's Len?"

"That's what I was going to ask you. He missed supper. I got home and the house was dark. I'm not used to that. I think it's gotten me a little spooked after last night. I just thought he might have said something to you—maybe about where he was going tonight?"

Baby started to struggle up in the bed. "I don't know," he said thickly. "I don't remember anything." He got his back against the wall, yawning as he pried the pillow out from under his hips with his good hand. "Probably went to Royal's." He squinted at his mother; she looked so tired.

"Nope. I called there a few minutes ago. Well"—she got up—"I'll get your pills. The bakery just called; I have to go in very early tomorrow." She grimaced at her watch. "So I'm going to bed right away—unless—are you really okay? Because I can stay up with you."

"I'm okay," he said, putting one leg at a time carefully over the side of the bed.

"If you hear from Lenny, wake me, will you? I shouldn't worry—it's not like he can't live his own life." She laughed a little on her way out. "There's tomato soup. I'll heat it for you."

He pulled himself up off the bed and stood unsteadily, waiting for his vision to settle. He looked around the room; nothing to wear but those scummy clothes of Dwight's. So he stumbled into Lenny's room and stole his bathrobe.

"Your pills," his mother said as he came into the living room, blinking against the light. "And your soup." She held a tray, waiting for him to choose a place to sit. He settled himself heavily into the couch, and she put the tray in his lap. She stood there, looking down at him, then nodded and turned half away before she said, "Oh, I got you a present. It's in the bag there by the chair. Wake me if you need me." She went out into the back hall, leaving the door open behind her.

But he couldn't eat. His arm was aching. He took the pills and then he picked up the remote and turned on the TV, volume very low.

But Baby was restless. He turned off the TV. He wanted to be at Royal's with Lenny, leaning over an engine and getting his hands filthy. He went to the phone, punched up Royal's on the redial, and stood there, trying to cinch up the robe while he waited through the rings. Royal's machine answered. Baby hung up the phone, shivering. The house was unnaturally quiet.

His medication was beginning to kick in again; everything was a little soft around the edges. He sat down heavily on the couch, and then he remembered that his mother had mentioned leaving him a present.

Somebody knocked on the front door. It was a sudden, loud knock, and it gave Baby a bad start. He pulled himself up off of the couch, worriedly glancing over his shoulder toward his mother's room. The knock came again, harder this time. Heart hammering, Baby headed down the dark hall, groping for the light switch. The lightbulb blew when he turned it on. The knock sounded once more before he could get the door open.

He found himself staring into what seemed to be an unbroken darkness, until Monkey turned around, out in the shadows on the front walk. His face glowed pale in the dim light coming from inside the house, seeming to float in the dark. Baby was unsettled, seeing the black of the Clan for the first time like that, from the outside.

"Lenny here?" Monkey asked.

"Why?" Baby said.

Monkey gave him an insolent look. "Is he here?"

"No."

Monkey grunted. "When he comes back, you tell him I came by. Tell him I've got something to show him. Something special for the party tonight." Monkey grinned, patting a pocket, obviously pleased with himself.

"What party?" Baby said.

"Oh, yeah." Monkey smiled, like he was just recalling.

"You wouldn't know. It's Clan business," he said. He turned his back on Baby and walked the rest of the way down to the street.

"What party?" Baby asked again, beginning to feel a nasty, creeping sense of foreboding.

Monkey turned around at the end of the path. "What the hell?" he said. "You're not invited."

"I know it." Baby clenched his teeth against what he wanted to be saying.

"There may even be a new crown prince after tonight," Monkey bragged, grinning hard. "Lenny's new, personal yellow."

Baby nodded, tight-lipped.

"Tonight at midnight, like New Year's Eve."

"Where?" Baby asked him.

"What's the difference?" Monkey countered, starting down the sidewalk.

"Please," Baby said quickly.

Monkey stopped. "Pardon me?" he asked, pronouncing it with mock clarity.

Baby clenched his fist. "I said, 'Please.'"

Monkey smiled, walking backward. "Under the bridge," he said.

"Under the freeway," Baby guessed. "Where it crosses the tracks."

Monkey pointed at him. Yes.

"And Lenny's going to be there?" Baby asked.

Monkey spread his arms, turning away. "Guest of honor," he said, the words fading as the darkness received him.

Baby stood on the stoop, staring after him. Then he looked up the street. Empty. He stepped back inside, closed the door, and made sure it was locked. He flipped the light switch up and down a couple of times, muttering under his breath. He went and made sure the back door was locked, too; then he stood silently outside his mother's bedroom. She didn't stir.

He remembered the present, found the bag by the chair, and pulled it open suspiciously. She'd bought him clothes. Of course she had. He surveyed the outside of the bag, grunted when he read the name of the store, turned the bag over, and dumped the stuff out on the couch. Two pair of Levi's, two T-shirts, and a sweater. Not black. Baby sighed. And then he started the arduous process of trying to dress himself with only one arm. He was cross by the time he'd finished.

He lay down on the couch and tried the TV again, but he ended up stalking around the house, absently straightening things up. The Levi's were stiff; he felt strange in them, exiled. He was cold despite the sweater, so he put the bathrobe on over everything. He hauled out his books and tried to study, but he couldn't settle down long enough to concentrate. The clock ticked away in the other room.

A car pulled up in front. He took a quick look at the kitchen clock, hoping it was Lenny, but the sound of the engine wasn't right.

A few moments later, there was another knock at the door—a more civil one this time. Still, as he went down the dark hall to answer it, he had to hunch his shoulders to keep his skin from creeping.

He hadn't expected to see Casey.

"Hi," she said, balancing on the bottom step, not quite looking at him.

"What are you doing here?" he asked, too off balance to be delicate. She flinched.

"I brought you this," she said, her voice a little husky. She put out her hand. Her face was slightly swollen and out of shape, as if she'd been doing a lot of crying, and there were two flushed spots on her cheeks. She still wasn't looking him in the face. He put out his hand. She dropped something into it, already turning to leave. His fingers closed around hers, stopping her. She looked up, eyes slightly narrowed, as if she were expecting to be yelled at.

"You shouldn't be here alone," he said. Another flinch. "My mother's asleep," he explained. "And it's late."

"Okay, then," she said sharply. "Sorry." But he still had her hand. He glanced over his shoulder into the hall, wondering how much trouble it could mean, having her in the house. Sending her away felt too cold.

"You want to come in?" he asked her, trying not to sound too reluctant.

"Not if you don't want me," she said, tears near the surface.

He stood aside, making space for her. "Come on," he said, giving her hand a gentle pull. The night chill came in with her; he felt it on his arms and face as she passed. He closed the door and locked it tight.

He followed her down the hall, squinting at the thing in his hand. It was the black-and-yellow wristband, coiled up sadly on his palm. "I'd forgotten this," he murmured. He stopped in the doorway. She was standing stiffly by the television, across the room. He lifted his hand. "Thank you," he said. She gave him the briefest nod.

Then the house was quiet again, the ticking of the kitchen clock distinct and hollow. She started to say something, then swallowed it.

"What?" he asked, not unkindly.

She looked away. "You," she said, voice gone wet and fragmented, "were a little in love with me for a while there. Weren't you?" she said. Her mouth smiled tightly, but the eyes looked sore.

He made a noncommittal gesture.

"But you're not now," she concluded. They were finally looking at each other, the whole room between them. He shook his head. No. Not now.

She nodded, looked away, blinking.

"The Clan," he said, wincing at the word, "may not have loved me much. At least they were honest about it."

She nodded again and lifted her chin, staring into the dark kitchen. "May I . . . ," she said, unhappiness thick in her voice. "I've been sick all day. And I need to say something."

He waited. She glanced at him and, finding him not hostile, she went on. "First of all, I used my best friend." She swiped at her cheek with the butt of a palm. "And then I lied to you. And I lied to my parents." She opened her hands. "Joanna warned me. She said I was being arrogant. And my mom did, too. Terrible things happened because of me and my pride—talk about moments of revelation. Now I have no integrity. And your arm's broken. Because of me. And I am so sorry." She made another sweep at her cheek. "I don't listen."

"It's not that you don't listen," he said.

She closed her mouth, staring at the floor.

He leaned wearily back against the wall. "Casey," he said softly, shaking his head. "I told you things I never told anybody. You asked me questions nobody ever bothered asking. And you listened. And maybe because of that, so did I." He shrugged sadly. "It's not that you didn't care about me. Just not as much as about some other things, I guess. People can be like that."

"But you were right," she said.

"If I was so almighty right," he said heavily, "why did I go with you?" He had to sit down. He went over to close the door into the back hall, and then he wedged himself into a corner of the couch.

She was watching him. "Because you wanted to," she said finally.

He cut her a look. "And by the way, just so you know, you were right about some things yourself."

"They threw you out?" she guessed quietly.

His smile was grim. "Lenny did." He flicked a finger at his empty temple. "Nothing turned out to be the way I thought."

"I'm sorry," she said. She was still standing there, look-ing solitary and rigid.

"Lying makes me tired," he said.

"It makes me nauseous," she said.

He smiled. "Me too," he confessed.

"Does your arm hurt?" she asked. Her cheeks flushed. It was a stupid question.

"I'm on drugs," he reminded her wryly. "Nothing hurts." She pulled a grimace, and he felt himself respond-ing. "Why don't you sit down?" he asked her crossly. She looked surprised, and then glanced behind her searching for a chair. "You can sit on the couch," he said disgust-edly. "It's okay."

She gave him another tight smile and sat on the edge of the cushion—as if she was scared, not sure when her welcome would evaporate. He closed his eyes. "Casey," he said, "we weren't friends before. That, I was right about. There was nothing—no experience, not even many words—between us. Maybe now we can start." She looked at him, hugging herself, face a mess. "If you still want to," he added.

She looked away and nodded. Then she sniffled violently.

"No Kleenex," he told her. "Toilet paper. Back there. Don't wake my mom." He closed his eyes again, this time against dizziness, listening as she blew her nose in the other room. She came back with a wad of white tissue. "Is she sick?" she asked, taking the far corner of the couch.

"She goes to work at five," he said, glancing back over his shoulder at the clock. It was ten o'clock. He made an impatient sound and got up to call Royal's again. He picked up the phone, hit the redial, got the machine, and stopped just short of slamming the phone back down. "Damn," he spat.

"What?" she asked him.

"I don't know where my brother is," he said. "And it's making me nuts. We always know—well, sometimes not exactly *where,* but he doesn't just disappear like this. Something's not right. I know it. And all I can do is sit here."

"You could go look for him," she offered, applying the toilet paper to the end of her nose with one hand and digging in her pocket with the other.

"I don't have a car," he said distractedly.

"Check it out," she said, dangling her keys.

He stared at the keys, and then at her. But he shook his head.

"Okay," she said, a little disgusted. "Then what are you going to do?"

He drooped against the kitchen doorjamb. "I don't know," he said.

"It's only ten o'clock," she pointed out. "Look, at this point, I don't think anything could possibly make it worse with my parents. They're going to kill me anyway."

"They don't know?" he asked, wondering how she'd gotten that face by them.

"Not yet," she said, avoiding his eyes.

"But you're going to tell them?" he asked.

"Of course I am," she said, a little righteously. "But I couldn't do it before I made it right with Joanna and you. Because once this all comes out, they're going to keep me locked up in the cellar for the next forty years." She went on dismally, "Which would only be right. I just hope they don't jerk me out of tutoring." She winced a little, looking at him. "Unless you don't want me anymore, in which case it really doesn't matter." She groaned. "I am in so much trouble."

"They're going to think it's all my fault," he said sadly.

"No, they won't," she said brightly. "I'll tell them."

"Driving me around right now isn't going to help the situation," he warned her.

"Like I said"—she gave the keys a persuasive little shake—"how much worse could it get?"

"WHERE TO NOW?" Casey asked him. They'd been past Royal's—the place was shut up tight. Baby had been directing her up and down dismal little streets for what seemed like hours, deep in a part of town she hadn't even known existed, watching for any hint of his brother. He'd told her about Monkey's visit. She understood why he was getting a little crazy.

"Okay," he said. "You know Blue Hanger Cleaners? Down just off Center, across from the library? He could be there."

"Okay," she said obligingly, and turned right. She didn't mind any of this; she was willing to haul Baby around all night. Not that she was so worried about Lenny—her impressions of him hadn't left her with any sense of his helplessness. "So, what did you tell your mom in the note?"

"Just that I was looking for Lenny," he said, squinting out his window. "But she won't wake up. She works two jobs, and by ten, she's dead in the water."

Casey drove down a couple of blocks, over one, went down Center another three. Baby murmured as they passed certain houses, certain streets, ticking off names, possibilities. "The cleaners is closed," she reported finally. The neon sign was dark.

"No," he said. "The night crew is working in there. Just pull in through the drive-up."

She did as he directed, stopping in front of the window. They waited in silence for a few minutes. Then she thought she saw somebody moving around in the dark behind the window. A light went on. A man came to the window and peered out at them. What he saw must have satisfied him, because he unlocked the window and opened it. He was a nice-looking man, dark-haired, early twenties, and he wore a yellow-and-navy rugby shirt that looked as if it had never been anything but dry-cleaned and steam-pressed.

Baby was staring at the man. Casey looked from one of

them to the other, and she finally rolled down her window, waiting for Baby to do something.

"Edmund," Baby said, either a greeting or a question.

"How you doin', Babe?" the man responded gently.

Baby must have realized that he was still staring. He shook himself slightly. "You look good," he said, sounding a little doubtful.

The man, Edmund, smiled. "So do you," he said.

"I didn't know you'd done this," Baby said. "Was it because of me?"

The man smiled at Baby, again—it was a beautiful smile, full of love. Casey had to look away, because this was really not her business.

"You have to understand, Baby Brother," Edmund said, still gently, almost apologetically. "I've got a life and I've got customers to deal with. They don't understand this stuff, and they shouldn't have to. I stuck around a lot longer than I should have because of you and Len and a few others, but when I saw the way it was going with you and Shelly, I knew it was over. Shelly has his disciples, so it's not like he's going to lose sleep over me. I don't think Len will probably mess with it much longer. Not now that he sees a few things."

"I don't know where he is," Baby said quietly. You could hear the strain in his voice. "Something's going on, Edmund. Did he say anything to you?" There was a little silence. Casey looked up, to find that Edmund's face had the same Clan look to it Baby tended to get when he was being wary. She finally noticed the white braiding he wore around his wrist, and things began to come clear.

"Have you tried Royal's?" Edmund asked.

Baby made a little groan deep in his throat. "You don't

know, either. But you weren't surprised about me. So you must have seen him."

"Last night," Edmund said. "He told me about you then." Edmund looked thoughtful. "He was as upset as I've ever seen him. About what happened. About a bunch of punks hurting you like that. He'd do just about anything in the world for you, Baby. I don't know if you've ever really understood that."

Baby and Edmund shared a long look. Casey folded her hands into her lap.

"So, what's he doing tonight?" Baby asked softly. "Something for me?"

"Maybe," Edmund said. "I know he's mad at himself. I don't like it, either. But I'm telling you truly—I really don't know."

"Why don't you call the police?" Casey asked Baby. "Whatever it is, they'll stop it."

"And they'll throw Lenny in the can, too," Baby reminded her.

"Still," Edmund said, smiling at Casey, "that might be safer than the alternative."

"This is Casey," Baby said, glancing at her apologetically.

"Don't let him get into trouble," Edmund told her.

"I'm the wrong person to say that to," Casey said, blushing up to her ears. Baby poked her leg.

Edmund looked back over his shoulder and answered somebody in the room behind him. "I gotta go," he said, turning back to them. "Problems. Look, you call me when you find him, okay? I'm stuck here till three with the crew, but after that, I'll come looking for you if I haven't heard. Okay?"

"Okay," Baby said, sounding like that wasn't much comfort.

"Follow your instincts," Edmund said, straightening up. "Nice to meet you," he said to Casey, and put his hand out to feel for the edge of the window. "Call me," he said again.

"I will," Baby said hopelessly.

Edmund began to pull the window closed. "Edmund," Baby said quickly. Edmund waited, hand on the frame. Baby looked up at him, suddenly shy. "Do you think—" He moved his hand, indicating his clothes. "Are we going to hang anymore?"

Edmund grinned. "Child," he said, laughing, "it's not like we went and got married or something. I'll be over tomorrow night, if your brother doesn't get his keister thrown in the slammer." Edmund winked. "We've got some cards to play." He nodded at Casey, then closed the window and locked it. The lights went out.

Baby was smiling quietly to himself. He looked like a tired little kid.

"Feel any better?" she asked him. "Because it looks to me like you're not exactly tragically alone in the world."

"I feel better," Baby admitted, rubbing his eyes.

"What do we do now?" she asked, finally bored with the cruising and thinking that he needed some looking after.

He yawned. "You go home," he said.

"Sure," she told him. "When *you* do. You're going to fall apart in another fifteen minutes, anyway—look at you. Running around like this is not exactly what the doctor ordered. You'll probably get pneumonia or something."

"I slept all day," he protested. But then he yawned

again—a very wide, uncompromising yawn. He dropped his head back against the seat. "Fine," he said. "I don't know what good we're doing. Maybe you're right. Maybe we should just go home."

"Uh-huh," she said. "But since you have absolutely no intention of doing that, what do we do now?"

He took her wrist and twisted it around, checking her watch.

"Ow," she said. "It's almost eleven. My gosh."

"I guess we could get a burger," he said, giving her back her hand. "If you've got money?" She nodded. He looked down at himself, one corner of his mouth drawn up ruefully. "It doesn't matter anymore, huh? I guess we can go pretty much anywhere we want."

"Anywhere but the drive-in," she agreed, grinning. She put the car in gear, deciding they were going to make a celebration out of this. They ended up at TGI Friday's, where she bought him potato skins and a gourmet burger and embarrassed him to death.

"You're spending too much," he kept warning her.

And then, of course, he couldn't eat any of it.

sixteen

MONKEY HAD BEEN WRONG ABOUT THE TIME.
When they got there, driving cautiously up a dimly lit street in the industrial section of town, Monkey's party had already started. Shapes were flitting in and out of the shadows under the bridge—black shirts, blue jackets.

"Put it there," he told her as they neared the bridge, pointing out a shadowed place. "Park your nose down that way—if we need to get out quick, we don't want to have to mess with turning around." So far, she was obedient. When she looked at him, he fixed her with a stern eye. "You stay in here," he said. "And you keep the doors locked. I don't know what's going to happen." And then he was out of the car and running toward the place, his hurt arm clutched tightly against his body. She didn't even think about it; the second he hit the pavement, she was out of the car and following him.

In the dim spill of the streetlights under the freeway viaduct, the Clan formed one side of a wide, broken circle, the jackets on the other. Jeers and insults flew, but none of that came from the Clan. Silently, they stood, focused on the two people who were faced off in the middle of the circle. Casey was sure one of them was Baby's brother, and the other, the smaller of the two, had to be Gene Walenski.

None of them had seen Baby yet. As he got closer to the circle, running up behind the Clan side, he started shouting. "Wait," he was saying. *"Wait."*

Lenny heard him and looked up; in that split second, Gene moved. He took a step and made a kick, just like he was doing a punt, except that what he hit wasn't going anywhere. Instantly, Lenny curled up and dropped to the ground. A roar came from the Clan. The move had galvanized them, and the place erupted into violence.

All this Casey saw as she ran, silently flying after Baby. She caught the bridge abutment with both hands and hung there, trying to get her breath.

Dickon's blue Honda pulled up on the far side of the bridge. Dickon vaulted out of the car, ran a few steps, and then moved back and forth uncertainly.

Lenny was still doubled over, rolling on the asphalt. Gene, wild-eyed, shouted something and drew his foot back again. Baby threw himself between them, yelling. Casey couldn't hear what he was saying, but it was clearly not having any good effect. Gene, shoved away by other flailing bodies, was beating his way back to Lenny and Baby, out of control. Without even thinking, Casey pushed away from the bridge, dodged around other fights, and managed to slip in front of Gene before he could get to Baby. She shoved him back with everything she had, screaming, "Stop it. You're not thinking. Gene, stop it, stop it." But Gene shoved her out of the way.

Baby was shouting behind her, and Dickon was yelling something. Baby's name. "Look out," he was saying. "Get out of there."

Casey was spinning back into Gene's way when she saw what Dickon was trying to warn them about. She froze.

One of the Clan kids had a gun.

He was holding it in both hands, and he was pointing it in their direction. Somebody shoved Casey from behind, and she went flying onto the street, hands and knees ripping across the asphalt, breath knocked completely out of her.

Casey heard a shot. She threw herself over on her back, trying to see what had happened. Baby was down. But so was Gene. And suddenly, it was silent. Nobody moved.

"Monkey," somebody said.

It was then they heard the sirens. Maybe five seconds later, a police car swung around the corner three blocks away, lights whipping eerily, siren clear and cutting through the night.

The kid with the gun turned and stared at the car for a moment, mouth open. Then he ran. He ran the opposite way, down the middle of the street, heading down the same road Casey and Baby had driven in on. He hadn't gone ten yards before another patrol car came around the corner down that way. The kid froze, caught in its headlights.

The car screamed to a stop and the doors flew open.

"Dump it, Monkey," somebody shouted. "They can kill you. They'll have to shoot you."

Monkey spun on his heel, the gun still in his hand.

"Get rid of it," somebody else yelled, pleading.

Casey pulled herself up slowly, heart hammering. Doors were slamming on the police car behind them.

Monkey dropped the gun. They heard it hit the street.

He stood there, suspended in the glare of the headlights. Nothing happened for a long moment, only the lights going around and around against the cement walls of the abutment. And then the officers came carefully out from behind the doors of the car, one with a pistol, one with a riot gun aimed at Monkey's chest. Casey could hear the sound of their feet in the gravel, it was so quiet. Monkey made one small sound, but he didn't move. The policeman with the riot gun held it on Monkey, steady and careful on one side, while his partner took Monkey by the arms and escorted him to the waiting car.

THERE WAS A lot of noise in the police station. Thirty or so people milling around, doors opening and closing, questions and orders and people talking on pay phones. Baby had his eyes closed. He was sitting on a wooden bench between Dickon and Casey, and he was deeply content. Casey's fingers were loosely wrapped around his wrist— she didn't have much skin left on her hands after he'd dumped her on the road.

They'd taken Lenny and Gene Walenski down to the hospital. So Baby didn't have to worry about Lenny anymore, short of having to explain everything to their mother. Lord only knew who Monkey had thought he was going to shoot. But the shot had gone wild, then ricocheted off the bridge, catching Gene across the thigh. No serious harm done. Baby didn't know where they'd taken Monkey, and he didn't care.

Now they were taking statements, holding everybody until parents could come and collect them. The older guys were going to be in trouble, Lenny and Holt and some others—it was going to cost them, disorderly conduct and disturbing the peace. But again, no serious harm done. Except that the Clan now had trouble to its name.

Baby was tired. Exhausted, actually. But he knew he hadn't done anything wrong, and he was at peace for the first time in a very long while.

"Baby?"

He opened his eyes just a little. "Skyler," he said.

Skyler was looking down at him, his face bruised and troubled. He reached out a hand, stopped just short of touching Baby's temple. "You do that?" he asked.

"Len did," Baby said.

Skyler nodded. "Edmund, too," he said.

"I know," Baby said gently.

"It's out of balance," Skyler said. "Something's not right anymore."

Baby lifted a shoulder and smiled at him. "I'm out of it," he said.

Skyler nodded. He looked self-conscious. "This mean you don't want me to come over tomorrow night?" he asked.

"Skyler," Baby said, "if you still want to come, I still want you to come. Are we going to work tomorrow?" he asked Casey. He poked her with his elbow.

"What?" she said, jumping, mired in her own worries.

Baby tipped his head toward Skyler. "He needs to take apart a carburetor."

"Oh," she said, still distracted. "So?"

"So, are we going to work tomorrow?" Baby asked.

"Well," Casey said, "I suppose that depends on whether I'm still alive tomorrow."

"We'll just say yes," Baby told Skyler, grimacing.

"Good," Skyler said. He sighed, looking over at the

duty desk. "If they're going to make me wait for my parents, I'm going to be here forever. All I've got is my sister, and she's at work."

"Don't worry about it," Dickon said, giving him a friendly nod. "My dad'll take you." Skyler took a long look at Dickon, then seemed to unclench a little. He sat down on the floor by the end of the bench and slowly pulled the beads off the end of his braid.

Casey stiffened. Baby followed her gaze. More people were pushing their way in through the outside doors, the first among them his own mother. With her, somehow not surprisingly, was Casey's mother. And behind them, Casey's father, shoulder-to-shoulder with Mr. Hall.

Not one of them looked real happy.

"Oh, man," Casey murmured, taking a deep breath. "Here we go. Fasten your seat belts. And it wouldn't hurt to start praying."

seventeen

"**WILL YOU KNOCK IT OFF?**" BABY SAID. "I mean it. Get your hands off."

"Did anybody ever tell you," she asked, faking to the right, "you are *really* hard to get along with?"

"I'm getting it just fine, child," he said. *"Don't."*

"*Such* an ego," she said, reaching over his shoulder. "I'm just trying to help."

"Where's your American Systems book?" he asked severely. "Go read something. Go read the Bill of Rights."

"Fine. Now you double-click."

"Excuse me?" He lifted his hand, looking blank.

"Hey, Casey," Peter said, sticking his head in the door. "Do I have something stuck in my teeth?" A clothespin dangled from his upper braces. Casey gave him a long, sober look. "No," she said.

"Thanks." Peter disappeared.

"The mouse," Casey went on doggedly. "You put the cursor on the icon and you double-click on it. You want to open it, don't you?"

"Use the menu," Baby told himself.

"That's not— Fine. Do it your own way." Casey gave

up and flopped onto her father's wing-back chair.

"Casey, remember that this is your father's office," her mother warned, coming in from the hall. "If he sees you riding the arm of his chair like that . . ."

Casey sat up and demurely dusted off the arm of the chair with her hand.

"Will you please instruct her to leave me alone?" Baby asked.

"Leave him alone," her mother said, juggling a pile of fat file folders. "Why? What are you doing?"

"Trying to type this paper," he said, squinting at the computer screen. "I just about have it done—except for this little bit of . . ." He moved the mouse, clicked, stared, flinched, then groaned. "And she keeps messing with the computer."

"I'm not *messing* with it."

"Look," he told Casey, "just at least wait till I'm done." He looked up at Mrs. Willardson. "I'll be here all night if I let her read it; she'll make me do it over again."

"You know you're welcome to stay as long as you need to," Mrs. Willardson said absently. She balanced the pile of files on one arm, opened a file drawer, and started sifting through papers. "How's your brother doing?"

"Great," Baby said, studying the keyboard.

"Hunt and peck," Casey sneered.

"Leave him alone," her mother said. "I thought today was the day. What happened with the judge?"

"She sentenced them all to community service," Casey said, grinning. "The judge turned it over to Mr. Hall, and he has them all at the hospital, reading to little kids. He put them in teams. Gene and Lenny have to do it together."

Baby smiled. "How do you spell *indiscriminate*?"

"Look it up," Casey told him. "Mr. Hall's thrilled because Edmund's going to help him write the whole thing up in a paper. Mr. Hall's thinking about doing his master's on alternative education."

"I like your mom, by the way," Casey's mother said to Baby, sliding the file drawer shut. "She's got a lot of grit. Dinner in one hour."

"We're going out," Casey said casually. Mrs. Willardson smiled at her very sweetly. "Just kidding," Casey sang.

"When you're thirty-five," Mrs. Willardson said, smile gone. "Maybe."

"Can you stay and eat?" Casey asked Baby.

"It's my night," Baby told her. Then he told her mother, "My mom liked you, too. Which may be the only reason why"—he hit a key and flourished his one good hand—"I'm still allowed over here. Done," he announced. "Print it out, and I can go home."

"Home," Casey echoed. "You really think so?" She smiled—a slow, luxurious grin—and patted him gently on the top of his head. "If you really think so, Baby," Casey crooned happily, while her mother sent him a very sympathetic look, "dream on."